Christopher James has spent a lifetime in education as pupil, teacher, headmaster and academic consultant; whilst enjoying an equally rewarding time as a keen sportsman, including rugby at a first-class level, county athletics, racket sports and road running; and all the time scribbling away at short stories, children's fiction, adult novels, factual narratives and miscellaneous articles and essays; as well as sustaining a bountiful relationship with a loving wife, three talented grown-up children and four distinctively captivating grand-children to date.

Christopher James

ON THE BORDER

AUSTIN MACAULEY PUBLISHERS
LONDON * CAMBRIDGE * NEW YORK * SHARJAH

Copyright © Christopher James 2025

The right of Christopher James to be identified as author of this work has been asserted by the author in accordance with sections 77 and 78 of the Copyright, Designs and Patents Act 1988.

All rights reserved. No part of this publication may be reproduced, stored in a retrieval system, or transmitted in any form or by any means, electronic, mechanical, photocopying, recording, or otherwise, without the prior permission of the publishers.

Any person who commits any unauthorised act in relation to this publication may be liable to criminal prosecution and civil claims for damages.

This is a work of fiction. Names, characters, businesses, places, events, locales, and incidents are either the products of the author's imagination or used in a fictitious manner. Any resemblance to actual persons, living or dead, or actual events is purely coincidental.

A CIP catalogue record for this title is available from the British Library.

ISBN 9781035895038 (Paperback)
ISBN 9781035895045 (ePub e-book)

www.austinmacauley.com

First Published 2025
Austin Macauley Publishers Ltd®
1 Canada Square
Canary Wharf
London
E14 5AA

My grateful thanks are due to my daughters, Carrie and Jessica, for their proof-reading, editing skills and general encouragement; to my son, Jamie, who has promised to compose a stunning musical score when the book is made into a film or TV programme; and to my lovely wife, Jan, whose unwavering support of everything I do has helped me develop the best parts of the man I have become.

Character List

(A painting by Brueghel the Elder entitled *The Hunters in the Snow*)
A busker, who plays by the side of the river
Angel Enrique Cortes, chief of the native tribe known as the Esperillos
Autumn Cork, a native Waspero, who forms a relationship with Mangas
Ben Parker, station master at the railway
Black Star, a native ancestor of Mangas
Bobby LeRoy, Mary's son
Calvin Canton, Marshal of Nosinala
Carson Wong, manager of the casino known as *The Chrysalis*
Colonel Wesley Harding, board member overseeing Border Control, Policing and the Justice Department
Digger Brown, mine owner
Dolores 'Dolly' Bellworthy, Frank LeRoy's mistress
Domino, an aspirational market-trader
Eve Horner, daughter of Peter and Polly, who is attracted to Bobby LeRoy
Frank LeRoy, Mayor of Nosinala

Gangs, various, called The Noz, The Second-Chancers, The Buffer Boys, The Jackals, The Esperillos, The Conchillas, The Wasperos
Hank Starling, a Border Control agent, the right-hand man of Colonel Harding
Hendrik van de Berg, undertaker and gun supplier
Henry and Olive Saddles, owners of the local guest house 'Saddles'
Jack Bonneville, the state governor's representative on the board
James Blackeagle, features writer at the Nosinalan News
Luke Pointmoor, deputy marshal of Nosinala
Mangas, Frank LeRoy's bodyguard, assistant, partner and friend
Mary LeRoy, Frank's wife
Michael Stead, an old flame of Dolly Bellworthy
Miles McKay, board member i/c hospitality and recreation and owner of the hotel *The Elgin*
Miss Agnes Benson, a local octogenarian eccentric
Molly Doyle, manageress of *The Sunrise Parlour*, a brothel
Perry Northrop, property developer, businessman and member of the board
Peter and Polly Horner, guests at 'Saddles'
Red, leader of the Conchilla Tribe
Robson Calhoun, writer, guest at 'Saddles'
Rondo, Red's son
Room 101—a ghostly space at 'Saddles'
Ruby Stevens, editor of the Nosinalan News
Sheriff Nail, an independent lawman working south of the river
The Boy Billy—a ghost at 'Saddles'

The Ferryman, who transports travellers across the Niba
The Old Gardener—a ghost at Saddles
The Old Lady, who starts the ceremony of the Lacrosse Festival
The Sad-Eyed Lady—a ghost at Saddles
The Skanze, a wind that blows
The Wanageeniba, the 'Niba', the river that separates the two settlements
Warren Clay, the state governor
William Hopkins, reverend of *The Holy Souls*, the parish church
Wilson Creek, owner of the local general stores
Winnie Crane, board member responsible for health and community care
Winnie Crane's husband, serving a life sentence for murder
Zac and Cheyenne Wallace, guests at 'Saddles'
Various other unnamed characters

And so, you might believe—like monks of old (and monks of today, for that matter)—that all quotidian life is merely a preparation for the day of one's death and that this daily, seemingly endless, narrative is nothing compared to the final moment of judgement that leads to true eternity. It is not a life ended, after all, but simply a life changed.

And you might just cling on to the deeply-held restorative that in times of conflict: under the mountains; beyond the woods, beside the towns; on the hinterlands between; at the edges along; beneath the blue-black waters; through the midst and the mist of bullets and spears; by days, by nights, by dreams, by nightmares; despite doubts and convictions; below the depths of guilt and above the heights of euphoria—along the borders of life—may all our endeavours, performed by those who have tried, protect and preserve us in days of judgement to come.

The mayor of Nosinala, Frank LeRoy, stood in front of the large print of Bruegel the Elder's *Hunters in the Snow* which he had brought with him down from the mountains high all those years ago and he was not an entirely happy man. The painting provided some kind of consolation, or inspiration, to him, he supposed, but it was an endless source of fascination and frustration, too. In the painting, there were muted colours in the pale green skies and the red-brick buildings and the rarefied redness of some of the dogs, straggling as they were in the rearguard of the company, as the flames of the fire shone, suffused, in the faces of the women, hopefully, forlornly, and these colours were contrasted with the blackness of the birds and the dark-brown, wasted trees, whilst the white snows stretched as far as the eye could see across the slopes and the crags in the distance. A solitary black bird was wheeling in the circling sky against the white background when perhaps it should have been painted white in a swirling kaleidoscope of stronger primary colours, but, despite this absence of hope—or, perhaps, because of it—the bird looked down, indifferently, yet with almost malevolent intent, on the human skaters on the ice below engaging with their own circularities, their own random joys, their own relief from everyday strains. And the hunters were returning, dejected, from the hunt with the heads of their hounds hanging low, their throws of the dice unsuccessful, their hearts and roles smitten by the vagaries and harsh realities of life.

At that moment, as Frank looked at the painting, he was irritated anew by the broken sign of the inn that hung precariously, almost unnoticed, in the left-hand margin of the picture and he was angry at the fact that nobody had bothered to mend it. In his head, he knew it was just a painting, captured in the moment, so any kind of repair was impossible, but his heart told him that things like this should not be so and with that disgruntled thought pulsing illogically in the hinterland of his perception, he moved towards the mirror on the opposite wall, fashioned his bow-tie into a suitable shape, stroked his hands gently round the outline of his neatly-trimmed beard and moustache and called out to his bodyguard who was standing by the door in the outer room blotting out the light.

"Mangas! I'm going for a walk round the town."

Mangas stretched his six-foot six-inches frame before reaching for his gun. When the mayor wanted to go for a walk, that meant Mangas had to accompany him. Mangas lowered his head as he led the way out of the office touching the top of the door frame for luck as he went. The inside of the door was painted red; the outside was black.

The mayor and the bodyguard stepped languidly out onto the streets of Nosinala to notice in the heat of the afternoon sun that not very much was happening. Frank strode confidently; Mangas walked with a slight limp. It was a relief not to be looking over one's shoulder wondering if this was the day that the shadows would fall.

Nosinala was an unremarkable small town situated just north of the River Wanageeniba, the course of which wound like a sidewinding snake forming a natural border between land to the north and territories to the south. Nosinala was nothing out of the ordinary except for the fact that there was another small town named Nosinala to the south of the river directly opposite its northern namesake. One could stand in north Nosinala and wave at residents in south Nosinala and there were some, but not many, who actually did wave from time to time when relations were good. When relations were not so good, there wasn't time for much waving of any kind; at such times it was best to keep one's head down. The river at the point between the two townships was not very wide nor fast-flowing so in the summer season, it was possible to wade across if you kept your goods or your gifts or your guns above your head. The river could be capricious, however, especially when in flood, and there were treacherous undercurrents further round the bends but in places where it was tranquil, it showed its gentle and accommodating nature, most of the time.

One could be forgiven for thinking that the early pioneers who gave names to their developing settlements were a little lazy or unimaginative in choosing the same name for their burgeoning settlement and that, at the very least, they should see themselves as two halves of the same foundation, sharing the name, location, laws and ordinances, as well as living harmoniously either side of the watercourse they habitually called 'Niba'. The name of their town was supposed to have originated from ancient dialects meaning 'black gold'—although historians and linguists dispute this—but both sides of the river rather liked the connection and saw it as a good omen. In any event, since there truly was gold and oil and black waters swimming underneath them in the soil and washing over them by the Wanageeniba, neither side was willing to give up the name so the designation persisted, separately, independently, and the cartographers duly obliged on their maps and the locals found ways to make it work even if they also found ways to disagree and argue on practically everything else.

Mayor LeRoy and Mangas had circumnavigated the few main streets adjoining their office and had strolled more purposefully now away from the sound of the railway carriages shuffling into the station and towards the banks of the Niba whose waters played such a central part in the two towns' identities and independent, yet related, fortunes.

Frank LeRoy liked the river. It was a far cry from the mountains some 700 miles further north from where he had entered Nosinala some twenty years ago. He had brought his Bruegel painting with him even if the sign needed repair and he had brought his good friend Mangas with him too. They had hunted and tracked and climbed amongst the forests and the mountain foothills—though Mangas would not ever go higher where the air was thin—until the time for such things had come to an end. Shadows fall. People come and go. But the tracks and traces one leaves behind are picked up by others who follow. LeRoy missed the mountain air but he liked the cooling waters of Niba and he quickly came to appreciate its importance as a central artery, like the aorta to the human heart, carrying lifeblood to the organs and tissues of the town.

When LeRoy referred to 'the town', he thought only of that particular settlement that had grown north of the river; all that lay to the south was not his jurisdiction. He had centrally appointed marshals who worked for him; Nosinala South had only local sheriffs who came and went, like tumbleweed, as well as the sadly irrelevant chieftains, despite their authenticity, of fractured nomadic tribes who roamed randomly even further to the south in those arid lands that yielded nothing but dust and discord. It was easy to fall under the spell of lazy clichés but those born 'south of the river' carried their disadvantages round with them despite the biblical strength of their Sheriff Nail who was proving to be anything but tumbleweed.

Nevertheless, their provenance rattled in their voices and you could see it in their eyes, almost hear it in the beating of their hearts. True Nosinalans were from the north; those from the south were known as 'Noz' and, if you were born 'south of the river', as in so many other places around the world, you had to work harder just to survive. It has been said of many marginalised places south of the river that the sound of the early morning police siren was just the usual wake-up call of the day.

Mangas, on the other hand, did not enjoy the river, and like many of his race, retained a superstitious fear about the gods of the Wanageeniba that went beyond rational explanation even though he was some three generations removed from his ancestors and their primitive beliefs. But what's a mere three generations when the essence of the spirit runs so deep? It didn't do to take the river gods lightly. Mangas had lived in the mountain ranges and had family ties in the deep south; it was the middle ground around the Niba where he felt less comfortable. Such misgivings were not so pronounced as to render him incapable of living in Nosinala these last twenty years but the ache remained and he felt it most acutely when his bones felt the pull of the waters, as they did now, standing beside the mayor, looking south. Although why his bones should feel the pull of the water, he could not fathom because Mangas could not swim.

Three figures on the other side of the river could be made out though they were not within shouting distance. One of them waved feebly in their direction. Frank LeRoy ignored the gesture, even if he saw it, but Mangas slowly raised his massive arm and acknowledged the greeting. By reaching towards the airy sky, he could exorcise any demons from the deep.

"It's a fine sight, isn't it, Mangas? The world, I mean, the river, the town, everything in its place. Niba just keeps on flowing, doesn't it, despite all the problems."

The mayor might have had a touch of poetry in his soul and he might have had the words on occasions like these but he couldn't understand what was going on underneath Mangas' skin and he had never really understood Mangas' spiritual point of view.

"Well, anyway, it's no good here standing watching the storks, though I'd like the river to be more green than turn that deeper blue," said the mayor. He was full of such random proverbs—for there were no storks in sight and the colour of the river was changing constantly.

Many of these sayings he apparently made up on the spot and Mangas had become accustomed to them. Besides, Mangas thought the river looked black.

"Let's head back," said Frank.

When they returned to the mayor's office the marshal, Calvin Canton, was there to greet them, as well as the deputy marshal, Luke Pointmoor. Frank LeRoy had never taken to his law enforcement officers partly because they didn't appear to have a grip on the rising crime wave that held the town in a poisonous vice but also because they were typical of the officious non-entities who rose to the levels of their incompetence. Plus he just didn't like their personalities. Privately, he called them 'Cant' and 'Pointless'. Sometimes he might have changed a vowel and consonant or two.

In fairness, the mayor realised that the causes and incidence of the crime endemic were far beyond the control of his unsatisfactory marshals but he wasn't above a little scapegoating for all that. And for all Frank's poetic liking for the river, he realised that the problem of crime stemmed from the Niba itself, in that its waters formed the natural border between the north and the south. All borders create tensions none more so than the So-No Border which ran for fully two hundred miles east and west of its central point where the two Nosinalas waved uneasily at each other across the Wanageeniba. The north wanted most or all of some of the south's resources—when they found them—and the south wanted all that the north had to offer without necessarily having to put the foundations in place. When the early pioneers had stumbled across the territories, they were attracted to the richer pasture land to the north and the easier links across the plains to other developing settlements.

Across the river to the south, the land was swampy immediately around some of the riverbank regions and the semi-desert in patches beyond that, so it was natural for the settlers to set up their camps and then their homes north of the river. Indigenous tribes to the south didn't seem to pay much notice to the newcomers at the beginning whilst all those other impoverished settlers, who found no room on the northern side or who were forced to cross the river by the more enterprising of the trailblazers, seemed to lack the strength of purpose or initiative of those more successful frontier men and women.

These particular southern settlers—those who would become the 'Noz' of successive generations—were of many different nationalities lacking the distinctive character and central cohesion that might have provided a unifying identity. And yet they developed a wiry resilience of their own which smacked of survival rather like the instincts of hyenas. And they had to become resilient because the tribal groups, in the end, took rather more exception to them than they did to the new people north of the Wanageeniba.

What turned these local skirmishes and niggling tensions into something far deeper was the discovery of rich pickings on the southern side of the Niba when oil, then gold and silver, and then other valuable minerals were found beneath the surface of that seemingly inhospitable land. The southerners had found their bargaining power and the northerners were not slow in claiming them for their own. The Noz found themselves being pushed further south by the Nosinalans but also squeezed by the natives whose nomadic and mostly placid inclinations did not extend to accommodating foreigners.

The battles raged to and fro. And so did the lines of demarcation. Treaties followed outbreaks of violence which were concluded by uneasy ceasefires and punctuated by sudden outbursts again. The representatives of the different parties tried to reach some lasting agreements and inevitably the strongest forces prevailed. The Nosinalans established the Niba as the natural border but changed the permanency of the arrangement whenever the river spilt its banks further south in times of flood or whenever the sites of new resources were discovered. The Noz resisted when they could but usually gave way in exchange for short-term trade deals. Even the natives began to taste the intoxicating fruits that sprouted, after all, from their own ancestral lands which demanded, in their view, recognition and recompense. The Nosinalans drew up sophisticated Bills of Human Rights declaring the integrity of 'people of different culture' and sent missionaries and educationalists to the tribes in the more-or-less earnest quest to embrace those 'lacking civilisation' even if their more fervent desire was to quell and control dissidents. This was the historical background to the crime waves that festered in both Nosinalas.

But Frank was less concerned with the history and more preoccupied with the need to manage and control the crime. The crime flowed from the river even if it was a little irrational to blame the indifferent Wanageeniba. The problem was smuggling. Smuggling of drugs, guns, gold, silver, precious cargo, people and all the attendant violence that accompanies such deviations. It was not the case that Frank did not care about the causes—how could he not when those in authority above him and other vested interests asked him continuously what the mayor of Nosinala was doing about it?

But when he delegated downwards and asked Marshal Canton what *he* was doing about it, the marshal just went out and shot another dodgy-looking Noz or two. So Frank felt he had no option but to look more deeply at the undercurrents. And he knew that his investigations and the solutions he would be proposing would not find favour with certain powerful groups who were sometimes made up of the very same people crying out for urgent action. He felt like the returning hunters in his Bruegel painting with their heads bent low, exchanging no words of warmth or welcome with their fellow citizens, committed to the thankless task, with no choice whatsoever but to fulfil their obligations in the dirty snow.

"Well, well, Marshal Canton! And you've brought your deputy, too! Have you some good news to tell me? Have you cracked open a smuggling cartel and imprisoned the gang-leaders?"

"Now, Mr LeRoy, you know I'm not going to say that. Besides, the prison's too small. I keep asking for a bigger prison, don't I?"

"Let's not get ahead of ourselves. Let's catch some criminals first. What news?"

"A section of the steel wall is reported as down by Yellowstone Pass. I thought I'd take a look at it."

There was a pause whilst Frank waited for something else.

"Well, then, Marshal," said Frank, sighing at Canton's lack of initiative, "Go and take a look!"

Frank watched the two of them depart purposefully and self-importantly and then turned to Mangas to say, "There go men who spill their porridge."

Mangas laughed.

Frank suddenly felt the urge for some love and understanding. He thought of the woman he loved waiting for him. He glanced at his watch.

"Mangas, if anybody wants me, I'll be at Cavendish Avenue. Why don't you take a break yourself? It'll take Cant and Pointless ages to report back. Who knows? They might get lost at Yellowstone Pass. I'll see you back here tomorrow if not before."

Mangas rose from his chair like a silent mountain and left the office knowing full well when to leave the mayor alone.

Frank got into his car, glanced down at the dashboard and smiled at the photo he kept there of his wife and son. He needed some comfort. He joined the main highway and took the road to Cavendish Avenue, to the suburbs, to the love he needed so badly.

The Reverend William Hopkins, of the Holy Souls Church, was engaged in one of his habitual tours of the town when he tried to reach out to as many people as possible, without judgement or prejudice, in the hope that his daily presence in Nosinala—and on earth—would not be wasted. He tried to become, as he put it, a 'kindly nuisance' but he sometimes wondered whether the people he encountered would have deleted the first part of that descriptor. No matter—he pressed on regardless. What was the worst thing that could happen to him? It would all be in vain, perhaps. Or he might get shot. Neither option would he have chosen but then he didn't choose to practise his ministry in Nosinala, either. But what would be the point of saving souls in some haven of earthly paradise? And what kind of vanilla life would that be? No, he was happiest amongst the people of Nosinala who were just like people everywhere, really, if a little rougher round the edges and a little rougher deep down, truth be told. Here were souls that needed him.

He met Molly Doyle who was perambulating on a kind of reaching-out mission of her own. She seemed to be receiving just as many friendly greetings as the reverend. Molly ran 'The Sunrise Parlour' where her ladies offered the time-worn services of old to (mostly) men whose needs were manifold and she, too, operated without judgement or prejudice. William Hopkins and Molly Doyle had more than once agreed they were involved in similar vocations even if at opposite ends of the spectrum. She nodded at several men as she walked by. Some of them acknowledged her, furtively; most scuttled quickly away lest they should be seen. Some women smiled, as if grateful; still more crossed the street whilst ruffling their dresses and skirts. Molly smiled, too, for, like them, that was exactly what she thought she did too—she simply rustled her skirts and her dresses.

"Good morning, Molly! How's business?" William asked.

"Never ending, William," she said, "Never ending!"

"It would be good to see you in church one Sunday, you know," said the reverend.

"One of these days, Reverend. There are plenty of mistresses and misers and malcontents already there, after all. I expect you have room for a Madam."

"There's always room for you. You can even sit at the front. I'll keep a place reserved."

"Thank you, William. There's no church I'd rather go to than yours. And, need I add, there's always a place for you at mine."

They fell to talking in less formulaic terms and enjoyed the fact that their friendship was a point of departure for some, a scandal for others, but always providing food for thought.

They talked about the weather and how people, like horses, behave differently when the wind blows. They talked about the town as if it were a living, breathing organism in constant need of succour. And they talked about the need to press on regardless. There was food to buy, plans to forge and the day to confront. They both had people to comfort—and souls to save—although perhaps only one of them dished out hypocrisy alongside the consolation. But then again, perhaps they both did that too.

The reverend waved across the street at Hendrik van de Berg, undertaker-cum-gun supplier, who suddenly seemed busy in another direction, and then he stopped to chat with Wilson Creek who owned the general stores. He made some purchases there. Wilson always kept a plentiful supply of candles. His local wines were also of the best and Reverend

William fully subscribed to the idea that any biblical or liturgical references to wine could hardly achieve sacramental value on designated occasions if they did not pass muster on a more everyday basis. Thus did his religiosity shimmer happily in the pragmatics of life even as it shone more conventionally on the Sabbath.

"I'll take some candlesticks, too, if I may, Wilson, and—since I'm here—why not throw in a couple of bottles of that interesting red over there? That's a new label, isn't it?"

"You're hot, Rev! That's *The Gifts of The Magi.* New in this week. It was meant to be *Jesus Saves* but somebody thought that just a bit too…um…sacrilicious. Is that the right word, Rev? I'm not too good with long words."

"Sacrilicious sounds just fine, Wilson. I might use it in my sermon on Sunday. See you there, I hope!"

"I'll be there, sir. Your sermons make my day. Makes me think, they do. Mind you, I don't know what you're going on about half the time."

"Well, I'm just pleased I strike home the other half then. Goodbye, Wilson, and thanks! Oh, hang on, those goblets over there…they look like medieval drinking vessels. Shall I take one of those?"

"They work out cheaper if you have six of them. And I could tell you that they date back to the time of Henry VIII of England except I can't tell lies to a reverend, can I? Plus I wouldn't recommend drinking alone, sir. What if the bishop dropped in? Or the mayor? Or the manager of the general stores of Nosinala? Take all six of them and we could have a rare old party!"

"I'll take six as long as you join me when I entertain the bishop and the mayor."

With that bargain struck, both men beamed and thanked their own versions of god for being alive.

Nosinala was going about its business because, like the river, that was what it did. The sun breathed life upon the inhabitants and the natural order of things took over, at least until the naturalness of things would be interrupted by an event or a mood that broke the fragile peacefulness. Such things were part of the natural order too so perhaps it was all the same. This was a frontier town after all. The border territories are often seen simply as places of movement where people and things pass through, move on and transfer back and forth but in amongst that inevitable activity these are places where 'the pause' holds sway, at least for a time.

Nosinala was a place where people could breathe for a while. A place where they could take stock, examine, think, investigate, recover and plan their next course of action. It might well be a place of violence built on fractures and wounds but it was also a place of healing. The town was going through one of its pauses. Even the air coming off the Niba seemed like a balm.

Reverend Hopkins inhaled as if imbibing from the chalice of communion and felt good about being where he was meant to be.

Mayor Frank LeRoy also felt comforted now that he had reached Cavendish Avenue.

He turned the key in the lock and closed the front door behind him glad to be back in the warmth and arms of the woman he loved.

Dolores looked up from the flowers she was arranging on a table in the spacious kitchen that looked out on her private courtyard and watered lawn.

"Darling! You're here!"

She rushed forward to kiss him.

"How's your wife? And how's Bobby?"

She never failed to ask him about Mary and his son. She always wanted it acknowledged between them that there were no taboo subjects. She wanted nothing to come between them.

"Mary's fine. So's Bobby. It's good to be here, Dolly. I feel like a hunter coming home."

Frank took off his long black coat and Dolly loosened his bow-tie. She also slipped out of her blouse thinking it more than slightly inappropriate not to show some pleasant enthusiasm on her part.

"No more hunting for you, my darling—for a while at least. How long have you got?"

Frank thought briefly about the broken steel wall at Yellowstone Pass and of the storks he didn't see at the Niba and a dozen other images that swam through his mind in an instant. He led her by the hand to the bedroom and made love with her for an hour.

Hendrik van de Berg had chosen to ignore William Hopkins' greeting and had scuttled back into his shop as if on important business. He really was on important business because he was *always* on important business not like that sauntering, ever-cheerful reverend who never seemed to have anything to do but talk. It was worse than that. The reverend intruded on people's lives, people's businesses, and just made life difficult. Hendrik didn't like the fact that the reverend could sometimes get inside his head; he disliked more the fact that this 'man of God' had the potential to interrupt the flow of his business. You'd think that the reverend of a town like

Nosinala would want to work closely with the undertaker, wouldn't you? That's what Hendrik thought.

People will die and undertakers are needed. Hendrik actually thought of himself as a 'funeral director'. He thought it was more in keeping with a society that had aspirations to be civilised. It gave him some integrity, some dignity. It had not been easy arriving in Nosinala with his parents from their own homeland all those years ago when people had to make a living. His father started off working in the blacksmith's forge but, as a boy, he thought the sweat and the heat of the fires unbearable. His father branched out to work with guns. There were a lot of them about. People always wanted guns. He developed a healthy business even if his methods of procurement and distribution were not always of the highest moral standards. Sometimes it was best not to ask too many questions. Hendrik learnt well from his father. He kept his head down and his business up. He became known as a reliable, discreet source and when his father died in a dispute over the very guns which had provided his living he expanded. And then more bodies piled up. Rough, hastily dug graves on the outskirts of town could only be a short-term measure for a community that wanted to be taken seriously.

The fundamental character might remain as a core component of any developing township but layers of respectability were needed to add a veneer of sophistication if a town was to thrive. He saw an opening when he overheard the marshal of the time clearing up the dead from another gunfight down by the river, "What we need is a proper undertaker!" Hendrik started up his business with immediate success especially since his customers were rather taken with the carefully attentive service provided by this new 'funeral director'. But Hendrik saw no reason to stop providing guns to those who wanted them. A man had to diversify if he wanted to succeed.

The reverend was a man who questioned the cause-and-effect of gun supplies and digging graves. He often urged Hendrik to reconsider the ethics of his business that dealt with bullets. The matter of death needed no encouragement. It required respectability. It was a rite of passage, sacramental, a time of peace, not a wrongful untimely end born out of violence. At least that was what the reverend said. But Hendrik raged. It was an easy connection for the reverend to make but it was a lazy conclusion that jumped over too many disparate factors. "*I* don't kill people," he exclaimed to himself. "Even my guns don't kill. They protect, they provide, they give pleasure to hunters and sportsmen." Besides, the reverend's religion had killed many more than those taken off by guns. Who was the reverend to lecture him? It wasn't as if he was the one pulling the trigger. He was more worried about the mayor whose ordinances were becoming increasingly restrictive about gun control. Licences were being issued with ever more stringent conditions. Inevitably, those with connections—the richer, the northern Nosinalans—got the guns; the Noz, who arguably had need of them most, lost out. The business was being squeezed. Besides, if all the guns ended up in the hands of one 'side' only, that just meant the killings simply multiplied on the side of those with guns. His way of doing business meant there was at least some natural deterrence at work. The proliferation of guns on an even distribution gave those with guns some pause for thought. So his reasoning went. It was easy to justify when justification was called for. He thought he would write a letter to the local 'Nosinala News'. Or he might just keep his head down.

Digger Brown nodded to Hendrik as he crossed the road and shouted out his thanks for the latest consignment; Hendrik bowed in slightly obsequious acknowledgement of the greeting. Digger was another local Nosinalan who wasn't best pleased with the mayor. Digger had worked his way up from the bottom like many successful top-line executives in their chosen fields and in his case his name had stuck with him from the very beginning because digging was his trade. He now owned the Nosinalan Mining Company that he had stumbled upon and created, literally, out of the ground for he dealt in gold and silver. He liked anything that could be extracted from the soil—as long as it had the potential to make money for him—and his lucky break came only recently but the fact remained that his discovery of the largest gold nugget ever found in the state, in a fast-flowing tributary of the Niba just beyond the railway station, meant that he could lay claim to the richest seam for miles around.

The establishment of his enterprise as an incorporated business and his proximity to good transport links by river, road and rail saw his fortune expand exponentially so that today, he was one of the richest and most influential entrepreneurs in the territory. And like many self-made men, he continued to roll up his sleeves and micro-manage his interests. And he didn't take kindly to the mayor's attempts to regulate his extractions on what he saw as spurious environmental grounds, nor the tighter legislation that was being promulgated from the mayor's office about monopolies.

He had taken time off from the workplace—from what he liked to call the gold face—in order to attend the meeting. It was the monthly gathering of local worthies who had started off as a guild with vested interests in the success of the township but which had broadened its power base and legality in recent years to form an official association that effectively regulated Nosinalan affairs. It enforced its authority through willpower, local muscle and influence over the police and justice systems. It established the Border Control Agency to manage the frontiers and it gained legitimacy from its recognition from the state governor. Those who were invited to attend called themselves board members but they agreed not to elect a chairman so as to better protect their mutual interests.

The chairing—and hosting—of the meetings was held in rotation by each successive chairperson who drew up the agenda. Board members came and went according to a majority vote at the AGM. Others designated could be invited to attend without voting rights. The state governor, who always had the casting vote in the event of a split decision, retained the right to attend—or to send his representative—which he did occasionally. It was never put to the test but it was generally assumed that the governor had the necessary powers at his disposal to force through anything he wanted. The board currently consisted of Digger Brown, Perry Northrop, Winnie Crane, Colonel Wesley Harding, Miles McKay and the mayor who recorded the minutes. The agenda was always the same: matters arising, two or three items for discussion and any other business. Sometimes the meeting lasted only 15 minutes; on one occasion, it went over to a second day. The meetings usually happened on the first day of each month.

Perry Northrop was a property developer, businessman and philanthropist; Winnie Crane organised health and community care and took responsibility for the land and water regions; the colonel assumed an overseeing role managing border control, policing and the justice department; Miles McKay was in charge of visitors, recreation and the accommodation business; and Frank LeRoy, as mayor, had every day, wide-ranging powers. It was his job to see through the efficient delivery of all policies. He was appointed by the board but the members had set up a modicum of democracy for the people by establishing three-yearly elections even if they had complete control over those candidates who would run for office.

Frank LeRoy was just starting the second year of his third three-year cycle and should have felt more secure in his post than at any other time previously but this was patently not the case. He had not made many friends, it had to be said, except amongst those who didn't really yield much power. The men and women in the street on the northern side were really taken with their mayor and if such things were determined by the popular vote then he might well have felt confirmed in his position but such validation, appreciated though it was by Frank himself, didn't make his life easier in the corridors and canyons where it mattered. *Uneasy lies the head that wears the crown.* For those on the southern side—the Noz—well, very few of them liked anybody, really, including themselves. *An honest Noz is like snow in the desert,* so went a Nosinalan saying, though sometimes such aphorisms become stories we tell ourselves in order to sustain the myths of our imagination like some survival mechanism. It doesn't do to challenge our prejudices with uncomfortable truths. The prejudices of life in these parts were constant, deep-grained and both subtle and overt.

Occasional outbursts of violence would make more obviously manifest the tensions felt in the different queues enforced in various lines in shops and at the border controls. Some people were stopped and searched; others would be waved on through. Quarantine of people, goods and livestock varied in length of days according to who you were or dependent on which side of the river you lived and worked. Forged paperwork would do for some and not for others. Employment, homes, education, rites and rights of passage, social benefits—all came under the scrutiny of the authenticated Nosinalans who sometimes didn't even know they were managing such matters with a jaundiced eye. It was a familiar story.

One of the stories Frank told himself was that he had no need of wider public acclaim, nor did he have need of stronger love as long as he had the love of Dolly. He didn't believe he had embarked on a sordid, selfish love affair, in the manner of most men who took mistresses. His love was honourable, his motives were pure and his transparency was clear. He had married Mary seventeen years ago and had provided her with love, security, protection and an increasingly comfortable lifestyle. She had enjoyed the role of mayor's wife. She was well-regarded in the community. She had been able to retain her own independence as a woman of leisure with intellectual and social aspirations of her own. He had even given her a son, Bobby, who was now 15 years old. Or so he had thought.

The boy on whom he had poured his undiluted, unquestioning love for a decade or more—and with whom he had the most wonderful relationship as father and son—turned out not to be of his making. One of several casual liaisons Mary had entertained over the years—this time, an itinerant poet of wavy locks and seductive verse—produced a boy whom Mary chose to masquerade as her husband's, especially when the wandering poet went 'itinerating' out-of-state, oblivious to the human progeny he had created with a measure and metre of rather more permanence than his dodgy poetry. Mary's subterfuge emerged one night in a drunken row and whilst Frank's love for the boy he had brought up as his son could not falter, his love for his wife died that very night, though he knew he needed to provide for the mother of the son, for in keeping the mother safe, he also kept his son secure.

Dolores Bellworthy did not feature for another year or more. She was not an act of revenge. Frank had resolved to stay with Mary until Bobby reached twenty-one. He reckoned that would give time enough for Bobby to become his own man, untied from his mother, and even, unshackled from himself who loved him as he loved his own life. And then Dolores settled in the town. She was a young widow. There were plenty of widows in Nosinala because that was what Nosinala did to women. All women were unique but Dolores was unique and different. Frank could do no better than compare her to the wind that changed the behaviour of horses and children. And she blew into his life and changed him too. His discipline, his morality and his inherent instincts to 'do the right thing' took a huge hit at a time when he was least expecting it. Dolores made all the people she encountered feel good. It was a gift from God. Or from the spirit that wandered the plains. Or from the ghosts of the river. Frank knew that he was not the only soul rescued or intoxicated by the spell but he fell headlong into her arms, her lips, her life. And the thing he could never quite understand was the intractable fact that she clearly adored him too. Her take on the matter was fatalistic.

"I was blown in on the winds to meet you, Frank. What do they call it—*The Skanze?* Let's not waste our good fortune. Let's enjoy it whilst it lasts," she said.

And they did not waste their time.

Frank wasn't a particularly religious man or an especially deep thinker but, of course, he was both of those things compared to the average man in the street. And his form of religious thought, typically, led him away from organised, prescriptive orthodoxies towards something far more esoteric and nebulous; he was attracted much more to Eastern philosophies. He was drawn to Hindu scripture, to the Bhagavad Gita, wherein the two precepts of *dharma*—duty and rightful action—and *jnana*—insight and knowledge—fought sometimes harmoniously but more often contrarily. He was dutiful, wasn't he, but did he possess a sufficient amount of insight?

In any event, Cavendish Avenue became another religious place, a true Garden of Eden before the Fall. Frank learnt how to live for the moment. He became young again, even innocent.

Mary knew that Frank no longer loved her and she even knew of Dolores of Cavendish Avenue. But she also knew when she was on to a good thing. She loved Bobby too with even more fervent depth than Frank did; she was the natural mother after all. She even loved Frank but she had never really found the words or actions to show him that. All she asked for was discretion for the sake of their son. She couldn't help thinking of Bobby as 'their' son. Over the years, it was a myth she had turned into a truth. The wandering poet was just a myth of his own. In her mind, he faded away like the wisps of a cloud in the sky with each passing year. From Frank's point of view, the presence of the poet lingered like a stain. Perhaps that was why Frank never liked poetry. So the three of them worked out an unspoken, yet recognised, arrangement—for the sake of the boy which seemed to work, at least until the moment might arrive when it would no longer be good enough. But for the principal actors, that was a denouement beyond their willing comprehension or control.

And life went on.

And so did the meeting.

This month's meeting was chaired by Winnie Crane and she had invited the board members into her home. Like all of the other members of the board, she had a large house situated in the protected and pleasant outskirts at some remove from the river and the railway. Her husband was not likely to trouble their business that day since he was serving a life sentence, without parole, for a double murder, in an out-of-state penitentiary. Her husband had been a seemingly respectable businessman who doubled as a serious drug handler on the side. Previously, police authorities had either not been able to supply sufficient evidence to bring him down or they had not really cared enough in the first place. But at least there was a kind of ethical structure behind his operations (if you can get over the lack of ethics involved in drug dealing in the first place) and his regulatory practices had had the effect of keeping a lid on things.

Winnie had been horrified to discover the truth of her husband's operations, as well as, of course, the murders he had committed. Her husband had normally instigated third-party courses of action when his business affairs needed the imposition of some discipline but he found himself at the sharp end one day and was drawn into a gun battle which led to him shooting dead an undercover policeman and a fifteen-year-old boy who had 'got in the way of a bullet' as his defence attorney put it in court.

Winnie decided to dedicate her life to the atonement of her husband's sins and took upon herself all the guilt she could muster, save that of moving out of the grand house her husband's dealings had secured for them both. Moral indignation can still retain some personal interest even if the hair-shirt worn is threadbare in places. Winnie went into health care. She devoted herself to the well-being of others and to the respectability of Nosinala. The board members thought that she would provide an acceptable face to their own aspirations for the town, some of which were not as nobly born as that of her own crusading zeal, and that she would be able to be 'managed' if ever any direct conflict of interests emerged. Hence the position we have reached today.

Winnie chaired the meeting.

All board members were present, including Jack Bonneville, the slick, sharp representative of the state governor.

Pleasantries were concluded over sparkling apple juice in her extensive garden at the back of the house. 'Matters Arising' were dispensed with quickly, once they moved into the study, as the main point on the agenda was the updating of the governor's latest scheme named 'Operation Second Chance'. This was a policy that had been implemented two months ago and which had been enacted with military-style speed mainly through the energies of Colonel Wesley Harding and his Border Control officials.

"And so we move to the 'Second-Chancers'. An honourable principle, Jack, but have there been any results?" Winnie said.

"Really pleasing! Couldn't have gone better! But I'll let the colonel provide the details," said Jack.

The colonel ran a hand over his neatly clipped moustache and spoke in a deadpan voice.

"We moved quickly following the last decision of the board. Hundreds of illegal immigrants were given the chance to accept the programme. We had a 95% pick-up rate. But why wouldn't we? It is a fair deal, a good deal for them. And we've saved ourselves a lot of hassle, plus we've freed up the holding pens. I'm keeping cattle and horses in there now!"

"Frank, have you anything to add?" Winnie asked.

"There are a lot more cows about, that's for sure. And fewer people, it has to be said."

"And the river smells more like a river again!" said Digger Brown, whose mining interests straddled both sides of the Niba.

"Were they transported carefully? What about the needs of those desperate people?" Winnie asked wearing her caring-for-victims hat. Besides, she felt emboldened since she was sitting in the chair, knowing that not too many others around the table would be concerned for the well-being of those who had been forcibly removed.

"We moved them quickly. Not too many questions asked. They were as keen to go as we were to move 'em. But there were no problems, if that's what you mean, Winnie," replied the colonel.

Winnie wasn't quite sure that was what she meant but she looked to the mayor with a quizzical smile that invited further elucidation.

Frank looked at the colonel.

"The migrants were moved quickly, that's for sure. As for repercussions, I think it's too early to say, but there has been no increase in activity in the buffer zones that I'm aware of. The few who chose to stay are now being processed through the usual legal routes and they are in temporary detention centres, alongside the cattle and horses. As for the families and any residual resentment…" Frank shrugged his shoulders.

Frank chose not to mention the portion of the steel wall at Yellowstone being down since he had not yet received the full details. He noticed that the colonel said nothing about that too.

"Oh, come on, Mr Mayor!" said Jack Bonneville. "Let's not be mealy-mouthed about this! By any measure, this was a successful operation and a humane one to boot. OK, we saved ourselves a lot of admin and the law courts are no longer overloaded but there are now hundreds of people somewhere else without a criminal record and a chance to start again. That's the point!"

Winnie could recognise the force of the argument. The intention of 'Operation Second Chance' was to cease prosecution of the immigrants—the 'aliens' as they were cruelly labelled by most of those who dealt with them first-hand—and provide them with safe passage to another territory, admittedly fully 500 miles away from Nosinala.

"My point is that we don't yet know the full impact on families and any subsequent problems down the line," said Frank.

"Well, that's as may be, Frank," said Jack Bonneville, "but, as you say, that's a problem some way off, if a problem at all. No, I think the operation has been an unqualified success and I take my hat off to the colonel and his team!"

The colonel nodded his head in acknowledgement of the compliment.

"I'll let my boys know you're pleased. They have a difficult job. My experience is that the aliens are not too free with their thanks."

Digger, Miles McKay and Perry Northrop laughed. Jack smiled. Frank and Winnie kept straight faces.

"Well, perhaps we've moved onto AOB, gentlemen. Shall we go round the room?" She looked to her left. "Perry, anything you want to bring up?"

"Nope. I'm just hoping the tourists flock in now that there are fewer undesirables about."

Miles said, "Amen to that!"

Winnie invited the members in turn to contribute any comments. The other points that were made were of a minor nature requiring little further discussion. Frank resisted the urge to express additional misgivings about the 'Second-Chancers' and the meeting broke up in quick order. Their deliberations were nothing if not brisk and that was to the liking of all.

Sheriff Nail lived and worked south of the Niba.

Sheriff Nail's take on 'Operation Second Chance' was more akin to the mayor's than the rest of the board although he did not know that. He was apprehensive about the consequences of moving the offenders 500 miles from their homelands. Their home territories were not much, he readily granted the authorities that argument, but they did have one thing going for them and that was the fact that such land was *theirs*. Ownership, familiarity and traditional ties counted for a lot for all people and with these men in particular. Not that they were just men, either; the new ordinance took in the fate of many women, too, who were just as desperate as their menfolk, perhaps more so. The sheriff was not particularly dismayed about the fact that he had not been consulted about the idea of 'Operation Second Chance'—he was used to being side-lined by sanctions from the 'other side of the river'; he was a Noz, after all, appointed by the Noz, for the Noz—but he could see that nobody would gain by this new initiative, least of all, the northern Nosinalans, who would not have seen the irony even if they had ever possessed any measure of sensibility in their souls capable of discerning layers of meaning, poetic justice, existence.

The southern Nosinalans gained nothing at all except, of course, temporary expediency. Sheriff Nail was an anomaly and his continued placement in the post, as well as his attachment to life itself, bemused and unsettled all parties both north and south of the Niba. He should have been dispatched a long time ago. A stray bullet would have done it. Or some political manoeuvrings. But Sheriff Nail, whose Christian name remained a mystery to all, including, perhaps, himself, survived, despite the tendency for sheriffs south of the Niba to remain sheriffs for about 12 months on average. The sheriff's chair he sat on in his ramshackle shed, almost directly opposite the railway station on the northern side, had now moulded itself to his formidable frame in such a way of apparent permanence that even the very furniture was declaring its attachment to this distinctive man.

Nail had been a bare-knuckle boxing champion in his youth and possessed a simple faith and philosophy that leant towards the clarity of metaphorical single-syllables rather than obfuscation. Sherrif Nail was firmly in this camp. A later boxer of some renown is supposed to have declared that everyone has a plan until he is hit in the face. If anybody had asked him about 'Operation Second Chance' he would have said that *that won't work*. In this, he would have had sympathy with the mayor's misgivings except for the fact that he did not know Frank LeRoy, personally, and for the more pressing fact that every ordinance that came out of the Nosinalan Board was presented on multifarious bills and posters with the authoritative signature 'By Order of the Mayor of Nosinala'. He had his reasons for despising Frank LeRoy along with many others.

Sheriff Nail was an Old Testament kind of guy.

One of the negative consequences of 'Operation Second Chance' was that it created yet another layer of criminal class more hardened than any other heretofore. There already existed the 'Buffer Boys' who lived from hand to mouth on either side of the river. There were the Noz, generally, from whose ranks any number and type might yet emerge on a whim or prayer. Or perhaps that should be the lack of a prayer. There were also the indigenous natives whose primeval, tribal connections ran deep. These new 'Second-Chancers' seemed to take on a fresh identity of their own harbouring less the welcomed virtues of redemption but more the rat-pack instincts of revenge. But it should be stated emphatically, however, that not all these disparate groups necessarily bred violence and lawlessness.

On the contrary, there remained, at its core, a level of decency and moral righteousness far beyond the levels shown elsewhere. But such factions inevitably produced their own disaffected beings and from such seeds grew apathy, then survival, then protest, then revolt. And alongside such transparent developments there festered and thrived the underclass who characteristically operated in the darker, secret, passages of life. Nor was the northern side of the river exempt from these phenomena. The 'Buffer Boys' transposed there and an emerging class of 'Jackals' translated and transferred and transcended and transmuted. The only things they did not do were transfiguration and transubstantiation. The 'Jackals' were the enablers and they fed off the weaknesses and needs of others.

Sheriff Nail hated the Jackals most of all. But his heart and soul were for the Noz and for the tribal chiefdoms. And the tribal chiefs respected him. They called him 'Iron Man'.

But Sheriff Nail clung on to his anomalies. And one of them was his daily attendance at the Mass of the morning. At eight o'clock in the morning, he was one of about twenty other parishioners who would silently and distantly from each other observe the protocols of Christian communion. The church was called *The Holy Souls*. It would do for him. One of the strange fascinations he clung to was the ritualised and attentively devoted way the priest of the day, and every day, would attend to the washing and cleansing of the chalice after communion. He watched with a mesmerised stare. This was ritual at its best, its most seductive. He wished he could wash clean the business of life—which fell to him to attend—in such a chalice with such a flourish.

And there were signs that that business—dirty as it habitually was—was already becoming murkier. Other territories further up and down the border line had not taken kindly to an influx of discontented exiles banished from the township of Nosinala. These men and women had no homes, no jobs, no prospects and nothing to offer their newly-enforced communities and economies. They found themselves herded and placed in detention centres very similar to the ones they had left behind. Furthermore, these distant authorities simply rounded up their own dissidents, whose temporary 'residency' in the holding pens had now been displaced by the newcomers, and packed them all off to Nosinala under the same 'Second Chance' ordinance signed by Mayor LeRoy. The principle—if such it was—at work here was 'What was sauce for the goose…'

Besides, the original Second-Chancers from Nosinala were also returning. A kind of injunction had been placed on them, to which they had been made to swear, declaring that they would never come back. But they really had no choice. They would rather face the authorities in the dark places they already knew than in other dark places where unknown dangers multiplied. The journey back was really not so bad. Travelling at night, stealing cars and horses, hitching illegal rides on random trucks, hanging on the back of passing trains which had stopped at local stations—all these and more provided relatively easy means of transport back to their homelands. And there was always walking. A man will walk many miles to claim his inheritance, such as it was.

So, suddenly, Sheriff Nail had a bigger problem on his hands. And so did Border Control. As well as the Marshal Calvin and his deputy, Pointmoor. And Mayor Frank LeRoy. And the good people of northern Nosinala. Things were hotting up.

And it *was* hot. A heatwave had descended. Sometimes, Nosinala was awaiting a storm or just recovering from one. Sometimes, it was just blazing hot. This was one of those times. The sun beat down like a lens seeming to concentrate all its energy on the town below. It was the kind of heat that made babies—and men—cry indiscriminately. Flies fell and flopped stupidly on window-sills and tables stunned and embarrassed by their inability to fly. Animals slunk away to find shelter and shade. Tarmac melted in wet tongues on the town's roads and the dust settled thick, then rose in eddies, in random flurries of wind, on the dirt-tracks. There was a palpable sense of irritation in the air. It was more than an irritation. It was undiluted malevolence gathering as a cloud. And nowhere was the heat felt more than in the buffer zones on either side of the Niba. People gathered by the river for relief, escape and even identity, but the mosquitos gathered there too and so did the jackals. The human jackals, that is. All kinds of carrion and detritus accumulated and festered on the banks of the river.

Miles McKoy was pleased that the sunshine had brought the visitors but not at all happy that the riverside haunts were being compromised. The holidaymakers liked to go boating and fishing and swimming. They were not going to be attracted by the intractable garbage, the angry aliens or the stifling inhospitality. His personal business interest was in the town's central and longest established hotel—*The Elgin*—but as Nosinala grew in importance and popularity, he built other hostels such as *The River Hotel* with views over the Niba and *The Waterside Inn* which catered for water sport enthusiasts.

He owned a couple of restaurants and diners dotted around the town as it expanded, and he assumed, by degrees, an overriding share interest in other hotels and leisure facilities that sprang up. He formed an association of tradespeople connected to the leisure and holiday business so that their futures could be protected and his role as a member of the board became crucial in consolidating and developing the local economy. *The Elgin* had its own gaming tables and he was forever trying to take over greater control of the many casinos that had proliferated on both sides of the buffer zone, many of which were managed by broadly respectable members of the Noz community, some even by the native tribesmen. He wanted to regulate these establishments, eliminate the rough crime that pervaded some of them and upgrade their appeal which already drew in many people from other states but also kept others away.

The accumulation of personal wealth was an undisputed factor in his plans but it wasn't just greed. He wanted fame, power, standing in the local territory and beyond. But it wasn't just those things either. He was a genuinely philanthropic entrepreneur who possessed an old-fashioned pioneer spirit that drove his ambitions which extended to the fortunes of the town as well as those for himself. Like many a frontiersman, he was not of local origin. His antecedents were Scottish, hence the name of the *Elgin Hotel*. He was proud of his Scottish roots and of Elgin in particular which nestled in the highlands roughly halfway between Inverness and Aberdeen.

Elgin had its own port called Lossiemouth and beyond that, there lay the Orkney and Shetland Isles which looked northwards onto not much else but the wide expanse of wild water leading to the arctic seas. Its history was recorded, after a fashion, on the hotel walls in Nosinala, perhaps as a reminder to visitors that the world was a big place and one's horizons should not be limited by the particular location one happened to live in. McKay had pictures of dinosaurs dotted up and down the hotel's main staircase—an *archosaur* caught the eye, a small crocodilian creature like a horizontal T-Rex—for Lossiemouth was renowned for its dinosaurs. Furthermore, the central lobby was dominated by a headless, armless marble statue of some Greek god in proud proprietorial homage to the 'Elgin marbles' stolen from the Parthenon.

Strange juxtapositions such as these made Nosinalan life richer, thought McKay. Men of exploring nature gained territory, artefacts and resources indiscriminately without too much regard for indigenous rights. The notion of ownership was flexible when acquiring, and only inviolable to the person doing the seizing when they came into his possession. But it was not all a matter of greed. Preservation, cultural development and the march of progress brought their own rewards, too. Indifferent, or even fundamentally benign, collateral damage littered the course of history the world over. McKay believed this to be the case regarding his own contributions to the life of the town. In what ways was he a philanthropist? He worked hard for the benefit of Nosinala. He provided employment. He built roads. He financed the railways. He brought in the tourists. And that was why he was exercised. He wanted the tourists to keep coming. He was right behind 'Operation Second Chance'. If people don't enhance their environment, move 'em on.

Chief Angel Enrique Cortes didn't understand the way such people thought. His nomadic tribes had moved on voluntarily, deliberately, as a matter of habit and lifestyle, for generations. There always used to be enough land. And sky for that matter. Angel and his predecessors accommodated the settlers at first even if it was a sometimes random matter of 'trade and raid'. But it was only relatively recently that the tensions had dominated. There were now too many apparently conflicting factions: the tribes (which themselves were not homogenous or harmonious); the Noz; the Buffer Boys; the Jackals; the Nosinalans; and, increasingly, the shifting waves of tourists, travellers, tradesmen and women who came and went. And into that mix now came the Second-Chancers, as well as the 'aliens' from other border regions. But his present concerns were with his own tribesfolk. Therein was the problem because they were not 'his own'.

The multifarious bands had different leaders for a start. They had developed different characteristics in lifestyle and temperament since different groups of them had become accustomed to living in the mountains, the foothills, the valleys, the canyons or the plains. They were adaptable but diverse. They even had different languages and dialects. Collectively, others called them the 'Navash' or the 'Navishi' but there were disparate clans like the Conchillas, Fancenzos, Jomondis, Buranos and the most numerous of all, the Esperillos, of which he was chief. When one factored in the many different treaties made over the years, all of which were made with due solemnity at the time but with the sole purpose, it seemed, of being broken, the political skills required by the chieftains rose far above the warrior fighting prowess also valued by the tribes, particularly by the young men. The women, of course, were drawn towards strength and stability, so 'might' often prevailed, but they did not necessarily subscribe to the archetypal roles of passivity and domesticity even if their contributions in those areas were vital. Some of the women warrior classes—known as 'Wasperos'—were as fierce and effective as their male counterparts and their hunting skills were nonpareil.

Angel needed all of his wisdom and strength to manage such a dynamic. The lifeforces that drove these tribes had their nuances but they remained essentially primeval even if there was a kind of fundamental and attractive spirituality that surpassed later supposedly more sophisticated creeds. He was of an indeterminate age which bestowed respect on its own terms as well as adding to the natural wisdom and authority he was naturally given, through his charisma, by the tribesmen and, indeed, by others, including the Nosinalans. It was as if the guy ropes of a universal tent were all pulling in different directions threatening to pull down the edifice rather than support and sustain. Angel was the tent master, the master of ceremonies and the uncrowned, but effectively consecrated, Grand Overlord. The Border Control authorities, in the person of no less a great military leader than that of Colonel Wesley Harding, called him the *de facto* chief of *All*

The Tribes and Angel Enrique Cortes was pleased to add to the nomenclature of tribal hierarchy this acknowledgement as 'De Facto Chief'. More than one potential dispute had been stilled by his declaration that the grieving parties should give way to his title, accorded to him by the great warriors of the north, as *De facto*.

Marshal Canton and his sidekick Pointmoor had arrived too late at the portion of the steel wall that had fallen at Yellowstone Pass. They arrived too late to stop the damage and they arrived too late to deal with the aftermath. That was what they did: *they arrived too late.* The steel wall in that section of the border line was still being built and somebody or something had caused a massive disruption resulting in a glaring hole in what should have been a bolted-on barrier segment. Debris lay strewn about the hole in the wall such as old tyres, bags of clothes, mattresses, packaging, wood and even white goods; on such things did some of the Noz make a living. The colonel's Border Control agents were already on the case and they did not prove particularly accommodating when the marshals turned up.

"So what's happening here, gents?" Calvin Canton asked in a kind of superior drawl.

The agents looked at each other and then turned back to the business of reconstructing the damage without saying anything.

"Looks like you men can't put a wall together!" said Canton, "Isn't that right, Luke?"

Pointmoor was enjoying the banter.

"I'd say these fellas need a lesson in wall construction, Marshal! 'Course, the real problem is they're putting it in the wrong place. Just look at that wet ground. I wouldn't put it there. No, sir!"

One of the agents moved towards Pointmoor as if to put something else where it shouldn't have been but a colleague pulled him back.

The truth of the matter is that this particular sector of the wall was indeed in the wrong place. It was closing off a natural access point between north and south. It was being built on flat, accessible land between two inhospitable ridges which also provided a valuable water source for animals and humans alike. If the wall went up, this would have necessitated a ten-mile journey east or west just to get across the border and then a similar journey to reach the water point. But this had been the intention of Border Control. Their strategy was based on major disruption of habitual crossing points for the Noz whilst funnelling such movements into easily manageable checkpoints with watchtowers, security, and the like. It was presumed that some of the Noz—the Buffer Boys perhaps—had sabotaged the wall at night judging from the ropes and the pulleys found scattered about. Repair was the first priority, then retribution. Examples would have to be made.

The Border Control agent who had pulled back his hot-tempered friend finally spoke to the marshals.

"We've got this under control. A little local difficulty is all. Tell the mayor we don't need another of his notices. Or another committee meeting. Now why don't you ride on back to town and let us get on with our work?"

Calvin recognised the colonel's right-hand man, who was doing the talking, as Hank Starling and decided it was better to leave with some dignity whilst they still had the chance to hold the upper hand. Plus, Calvin didn't want to start getting his hands dirty in building a wall.

"We'll leave you boys to it. We've got more important things to do anyway. Come on, Luke, let's clear out a few aliens along the buffer zone."

The marshals drove away rather pleased with themselves.

The border lines were established for hundreds of miles in both directions from this point, sometimes with natural barriers like the Niba and sometimes with man-made constructs like the wall, even if, in places, it was just a few strands of wire or more fragile wooden fences. The resulting lines of people crossing the boundary via the official checkpoints grew longer as a result but at least they provided some controls. Surveillance intensified in the form of agents, cameras and even roaming helicopters occasionally. Legitimate movements of goods and people from south to north were permissible, however, and it flowed both ways. Those from the south provided cheap labour and occasionally useful skills; those from the north travelled south in search of cheaper goods. But there was an active illegal trade in guns, drugs, slaves and precious minerals and jewels. Containment seemed to be the overriding policy rather than elimination. At least on this point, grim reality applied.

Environmentalists, educationalists and social workers tried hard to consider far-reaching strategies, but more often than not, the enforcers with the most success were the agents and the police. But the smugglers didn't really want to be helped by those who would otherwise right the wrongs. They thrived on the business of crime. And there grew up another class called the Jackals who preyed on the desperate needs of the disadvantaged by offering shelter, 'safe passage', false documents and starter packs for those seeking new lives in the more prosperous north. The cheaper goods sought by the northerners revolved around horses, cars, weapons, alcohol and, perhaps oddly, prescription drugs and medical supplies. Health care was a privately run business that was extremely expensive north of the border. Apart from paying a lot of money, northern Nosinalans had to join long waiting lists. They had to take evening appointments because people were working on other things during the day. And only certain approved drugs were available on prescription.

In southern Nosinala, there was less regulation. One could shop around because of the vast number of chemist stores and medical facilities available which drove prices down especially since the system was based on cash and on bartering which was the way of the Noz. The chemists and the doctors and the dentists south of the border had been trained and had qualified after a fashion and they had access to a full range of regular prescription drugs as well as quite a few other interesting varieties based on local concoctions that had not necessarily been processed through official routes but were no less effective and potent for all that. Patients arriving from the north sacrificed the luxurious clinics and the anterooms and the after-care but the whole exercise became slick in its rawness. All one had to do was exercise a degree of caution as to whose services one used and rely on recommendations and instincts. Plus there were some excellent practitioners there who preferred the variety of professional experiences such encounters offered. The regular Noz were amongst the healthiest people around; it was only that large wedge of less fortunate people living on the margins, lacking the resources to afford much of anything, who suffered disproportionately.

Throw in the casinos and the basic brothels and the corrals, where the wild horses were kept, and the used car lots and the flourishing open-air markets, where bargains could be picked up without too many questions being asked, and you had the vibrancy of a quick-fire supply-and-demand economy which worked well enough for some. There was also an artisan quarter where craftsmen and women worked on their tapestries and artifacts by day and sipped wine creatively with each other, or happily alone, at night, for the town was not devoid of art; on the contrary, the river, the railway, enticed a mixture of romantics and realists to set up their easels and kilns and bookstores to establish small studios where their works could be fashioned and displayed.

Push on through the buffer zone and Nosinala South was not as bad as the fastidious northerners sometimes thought, but such wrongheadedness has always been the case—as it was for Elizabethan genteel ladies with nosegays at the theatre, say (who were more likely to die at the hands of their lovers than from hoi-polloi below). Some people will not tolerate the pungent smells of life. Fortunately for the populace at large—and for the future generation of our humanity—the olfactory senses develop a resilience of their own, made more irrepressible by the increasing rate of occurrence.

But oftentimes, events have a greater immediacy on the actors of the moment. Not for them the objectivity of art or the reflective history and myth of place or the measured strategies of those capable of manipulating lifestyles. It was more usual for circumstances, even happenstances, to occur randomly, without connection or preamble. Poets often say that their writings don't have meaning, they just *are*. Perhaps this is the same for all the narratives of life. There is no interconnectedness. Except, contrarily, for the interface where points of intersection meet in a moment of thrilling encounter. Frank LeRoy could meet his epiphany by staring at his painting of *The Hunters*. Chroniclers and sociologists might want to immerse themselves in the recording and analysis of stories of the past. Trailblazers, movers, shakers and influencers might well believe that their orchestrations and exploitations of the trends of the time are 'on-point', most relevant and significant *sui generis*.

But Mangas—*Big Man Limping*—*Mangas*—the slow—*Mangas*—the mountain man who could not climb—and *Mangas*—the man of the river who could not swim—played his part in the pageantry left of centre, even off-stage.

Two children, a girl and a boy, had slipped away from the occasionally watchful gaze of their mother and had found a small canoe tethered to a wooden stake beside the river. The rope that held the canoe to the bank was flimsy and as the children jumped about inside the canoe the loose knot worked itself free. Their movements thrust the boat away from the hard gravel and onto the water. The children giggled but were not frightened. The water was shallow and they could see the riverbank. They could even see the other side of the river. The boy splashed his arms in the water and the girl did the same on the other side of the canoe. Before long, they were further out and the water was deeper though they could still see the river bottom. The girl then discovered two large paddles half-hidden under a section of tarpaulin in the bottom of the boat. They started to use them, after a fashion, and they were surprisingly effective as they pulled away further into the middle stretch of the Niba.

The boy stood up, more confident now, and started showing off with long thrusts of the paddle until he lost his balance and then lost control of the oar itself which fell into the river. He collapsed into the boat and a cut opened immediately on his knee. The girl watched the oar slip past her grasp. She leant over to haul it back in and in so doing, lost control of her own oar which also fell over the side. She screamed. Two oars now floated away from them. The boy laughed and then stopped laughing when he realised they were now in the deepest middle part of the river and the current was running more strongly taking them straight downstream into the faster-flowing waters. They could not see the riverbed bottom any longer. The wound in his knee hurt and he cried. The girl looked over to the other side of the river and thought she saw people waving but they were actually beckoning them to come in closer.

Back on the side of the river where they had started off, she could make out the figure of her mother who was now frantically waving her own arms and shouting something she couldn't quite hear. The girl wanted to cry but her brother was doing that. Mangas, on the bank, saw the mother in her agitation and knew he had no option; he would have to go in. He knew he could not swim so he began running in the shallows, limping in his familiar way, and then taking larger strides as the river rose up past his thighs to his waist and then his chest. He carried his arms high above his head as he had seen countless others do when they had made their carefully measured routes across the river at its most navigable point. But the children had drifted away from that safe passage and were in danger of being swept away past the bend. Mangas was strong and his steps were sure. His massive frame was gaining on the boat. The water was lapping his chin now but he could almost reach out and touch the point of the canoe in which the children were now clutching each other, whimpering, with wide eyes the size of squid.

One more step and he had managed it—he had grabbed the canoe and arrested its wayward movement. It was simpler, Mangas thought, to push on through this deepest part of the river and head for the other bank opposite. His strong legs continued to make good ground as he steered the boat towards shallower waters; the going became easier. The children had calmed a little but still shivered with fright. Mangas could see the figure of Sherrif Nail standing in the river up to his knees poised to ease them out. The two men easily brought the canoe safely in and a native woman stood there with a couple of blankets. She wrapped the blankets around the children once they had reached dry ground and she crushed some leaves of the yarrow plant growing by the riverbank to apply as a kind of poultice to the boy's knee. She also showed them how to chew the yellow flowers of the chamomile and then spit out the pulpy remains which left a pleasant apple flavour in their mouths which seemed to calm them even more.

Mangas wondered later, in his dreams, whether or not she had injected cannabis into their veins, though even the dream seemed unlikely. The mother on the opposite side had become calm, too, as she saw her children being towed to safety. She could see from afar the adults attending to the children who were being placed in a sturdier boat which was beginning to make its way back across the river, rowed by another man who had come onto the scene. The new boat carried the children and Mangas, all wrapped now in blankets. Sheriff Nail and the woman watched from the side. The children were shivering, then warming, then smiling and waving to their mother who wanted to hug them and chastise them at the same time. She threw her arms around them when they finally landed safely, panting with tears in her eyes, even if the dangers were more imagined than real.

The Niba might have taken hold of them and swept them off into the deeper, fast-moving currents had they been allowed to continue drifting but there was still some distance to go round the bend of the river at that point before such trickier waters were encountered and Mangas—the Steady—was always going to reach them in good time. The mother turned her attention to Mangas thanking him profusely for what she called his 'heroics'. He walked on, embarrassed, wanting to get out of the wet clothes. He encountered the marshals on his way up from the river who just laughed at the state of him and when news reached Frank LeRoy later that same day, his friend, the mayor, simply said to him, "Mangas, I applaud your attempt to learn how to swim. Next time, try it with your clothes off."

But the remnants of the incident weren't finished. Mangas met the mother and her two children shopping on the main street a few days later. The girl had spent some time at one of the market stalls that sold trinkets and beads. She walked up confidently to Mangas and gave him a necklace with an emblem in the shape of a snake—*Wanageeniba*, the river snake—and she whispered, "Thank you."

He put it round his neck saying, "Thank you, too. It will protect me. We are river gods now, you and I."

The story of Mangas and his river experience did not reach the *Nosinalan News*. Ruby Stevens, the editor, was not failing in her duty, even if her reporters were, but the kind of news that sold her papers was a heady mix of national, state and local items that warranted attention from the national, state and local dignitaries who essentially paid for and subscribed to her publications.

Nevertheless, the newspaper had a quirky, liberal-leaning which welcomed articles slightly off-beam; it was here that she thought she could deliver the eccentric and the specific. A typical letter might read like this:

I have long made a point of collecting mud from the river. I don't mean for the shells or the fossils but for the mud itself. I use it to ease the pain in my muscles tired. And for face-packs. And for making small bowls and vases. Sometimes it fills the cracks around the house. The mud on the Noz side is best. And there's plenty of it to go around. So my point is this: we shouldn't be too quick to put other people down.

Some people had no time for this kind of nonsense but Ruby Stevens loved it and felt that just the very publication of such sentiments provided her newspaper with authenticity. She reasoned that if she printed stuff like this, the very validity of *that* particular viewpoint—for you couldn't make it up—enhanced the authority of her editorials or other reportage on issues that 'mattered more'. She was pragmatic, if not altogether lacking in romance. The mud-gathering philosopher might have contested whether other essential subjects mattered more.

She had commissioned her features writer to embark on a series of *Profiles On…*She had to include the mayor and the 'Good and the Great', of course—especially Governor Warren Clay—but she liked to throw in the occasional oddball like Miss Benson and Sherriff Nail and especially Chief Angel Enrique Cortes if she could ever track down the latter amongst his horses and his women and his mystical plains. She was interested in the chief most of all.

She had already personally featured Colonel Wesley Harding and Perry Northrop. But she had given free rein to her features editor to produce something on Miss Benson. It elevated both her employee and Miss Benson. Her features editor, James Blackeagle, craved attention, publicity and validity—characteristics, she thought, which verged on the virtuous, given their professions.

"James," she said, one day, "Why don't you find a local eccentric? I could give you the names of several but find your own. Interview, research and write. Let's have something ground-breaking. Something that will make our readers sit up and take notice. Write it as if you care. Write it *because* you care. Then you can take on most of the *Profiles* from here on."

Blackeagle needed no second invitation. He had to balance the demands of a deadline with the integrity of the piece. He didn't want to profile yet another 'self-made man'. He didn't want a vital cog. He chose instead Miss Benson. This is what he wrote and this is what was published, unedited by Ruby Stevens.

THIS MONTH'S PROFILE—MISS AGNES BENSON

It has been said that people writing about old age adopt one of two stances. Either they take the point of view of nostalgia and regret, looking back with softly-watering, rheumy eyes or they rage against the dying of the sun by taking on ridiculously challenging mental and physical exertions as if to prove that there's life in the old trout yet. How sad and predictable it would be if the elderly always fell into one or other of these two camps. Agnes Benson—Miss Benson, if you please, to you and me—realised that one should not be sans teeth, sans eyes, sans taste, sans everything since such without-ness robbed one of certain fundamental sensations liable to confer, all things being equal, a reasonable measure of potential, but she had resolved to live her later years as if she was forever 45. She thought that that was about the right kind of age to enjoy sex without the messiness of misunderstanding. She thought that 45 bestowed wisdom without white hair.

She thought that she could still run, still read, still sing, still expect her voice to be heard and still shimmer down the walkways of life without concessions, allowances or patronage. She could still pull a trigger, as her daddy used to say. The fact that she was actually 85 didn't bother her because it didn't bother anybody else. The only eccentricity she allowed herself—which she had previously denied her youthful self—was the studious smoking of cigars on the grounds that health considerations didn't really matter anymore. In fact, she wished she had taken up smoking earlier. That was about the only regret and the only wild challenge in which she indulged.

"When did you start smoking?" I asked.

"When I reached my 75th birthday," she replied.

"And why start then?" I asked, not unreasonably, I thought.

*"That's a stupid question," she replied. It was then I thought that I should up my game. Miss Benson should be running a small country. Or a large one. But such countries do not deserve her. Nor can they afford her. Her experience is priceless. But what did she **do** with her life, I hear you ask? Well, she **did** and she **does**. What more does anybody want?*

There were other biographical details written out in a chronological list but the tone had been established by the account James Blackeagle had written.

From Miss Benson to the railway. The steel tracks were to the land what the river was to the, well, land. There were all the usual pragmatics, of course, like communication channels, transportation of goods, human interactions, etc, but there was also the sometimes forgotten subject of aesthetics. There was a kind of beauty about the Nosinalan Railway. The sights, the sounds and the smells of the railway created a particular brand of joy in those who appreciated such things.

The main station was situated by the river and the depot was just beyond that. It was opposite the depot that Sheriff Nail's shed sat almost within reach of a stone's throw. It would have had to have been a very good throw but it was close enough to see and be seen. The comings and goings of activity could be monitored: trains, carriages, workers, travellers and those who would cross the river at this point. Some people walked it, rather like Mangas with their arms held high above their heads. If Nail didn't think you should be crossing the river, he wouldn't let you; sometimes, he could be persuaded with a suitable fee. Sometimes he stopped you because that was his job.

And the ferryman—the same who had taken the children and Mangas across the Niba back to the mother—would also take you across—if your journey was legitimate—on his larger boat which was kept moored nearby for the purpose. Border control was not terribly exercised on the northern side because the crossing was so transparent and the flow of people was made up of recognisable persons designated as approved workers making every day two-way passages. But at night, when defences were down this particular point in the river provided yet another possible route for those desperate enough to escape from the south. Crossing safely and unseen was only the start of their problems, however. If they had walked over in the dark or even swum, where the river became deeper, they would, of course, be wet when they arrived at the other side, thus drawing attention to themselves. Some had tried to swim the distance underwater but some such migrants were often not seen again. Some would walk it naked with their clothes held in a bundle above their heads but even if they avoided the tell-tale sign of being dripping wet they still had to make the next stage of their journey onwards. The trains were an obvious option but here at the depot, and the station beyond, security was tighter.

The depot consisted of a few wooden raised shacks next to various tracks running in different directions away from the stockyard and warehouses that were dotted behind. A few ancient trucks battered and even broken rested behind one of the sheds. There was an assortment of loose planks, barrels and bags piled high to one side. Another dusty track led off to the mines that were still being worked on both sides of the river further downstream. About a mile to the west of the depot, there was a road and rail bridge across the Niba which dealt principally with railway traffic. The main two lines at the depot connected with the station the buildings of which were grander, even rather stately.

The station house itself was a large rectangular-shaped mostly red-brick building with a clock tower built into its edifice and red-ochre railings had been erected around the sides. It was separated from the railway track by a boardwalk which allowed plenty of access for deliveries and passengers. Inside, there was an enclosed waiting room with brown leather bench seats and also a rudimentary refreshment area dispensing drinks and pies. Ben Parker was the station master and he was deemed sufficiently important to be invited to attend board meetings occasionally though he had no voting rights. He was proud of his station and he kept his team working hard to high standards. Beyond the station, a short walk towards town would take the visitor to the open market stalls which supplied all sorts of useful and useless items although the traders could not always tell which category into which their goods fell. Their experience was that the locals, the tourists and the well-to-do from out of town liked high-quality goods, bargains and rubbish in equal measure.

Ben Parker did not like the mayor. He was fed up with what he saw as unnecessarily minute interventions in the routine organisation of the railway. *His* railway. The mayor's office was responsible for sending our new directives all the time affecting stock controls, movement of goods and even, sometimes, the timetable of trains and trucks in and out of the station. The station worked best when it was left to those who knew how to run things. That was Ben Parker—according to Ben Parker. The mayor had any number of clerks whose main function seemed to be that of posting bills around the town and down by the station announcing initiatives which amounted to restrictions. They were all signed off by Mayor Frank LeRoy.

Ben ambled away from the station on his way to town to take lunch with anybody he could find and he stopped off casually at the marketplace on his way through. There was the usual collection of hats, rugs, blankets, braids and buttons. He picked up a candlestick, then examined an old clock in more detail, before showing greater interest in some windchimes whose tinkling sounds resonated with him for some reason.

"Come on, Ben, buy the wind chimes. I can do a good price!" said one of the market-traders.

"No, thank you, matey. I have enough bells ringing in my head. But you haven't got the embalmed head of a crocodile have you, by any chance?"

Ben knew that the crocodile head was never going to be sold judging by the length of time it had been on display.

"You might joke but I bet I'll sell it soon," said the trader whose name was Domino. "I've now opened up the jaws. Would you look at those teeth? Why wouldn't somebody want it on their hallway table?"

Ben lingered for a while mostly moaning about the mayor's regulations and Domino joined in freely since all their trading activities were being monitored in ways that had not been the case previously. The mayor's office was now wanting to see 'certificates of ownership' for the items they were selling. The chances of Domino's suppliers being brought to heel by such measures were as slim as Domino retiring as a millionaire next week. Not that Domino didn't have such aspirations. Domino was a wild one and there was nothing he would not consider in order to realise his ambitions but he wasn't even close to his first thousand dollars let alone a million.

"But, Mr Ben Parker from the railway station, you should keep in with me because if anyone can make it here it'll be me! Remember Domino! One day, *I'll* be mayor!"

"But then who would sell the crocodile heads?" Ben laughed.

"Oh, I'll still be doing *that*. You see that's where the present mayor is going wrong. If you see him, just ask *him* how many crocodiles he's sold in the last year."

Ben almost asked Domino the same question but he didn't want to deflate his young friend's enthusiasm.

Ben sauntered on into town and met Hendrik van de Berg loitering by the *Elgin Hotel.*

"Hendrik, my friend," said Ben, cheerily. "Let me give you the chance to buy me that beer you promised."

Hendrik didn't remember any such promise—he would have been the last man to buy anybody a beer willingly—but he went with Ben to the bar in *The Elgin* nevertheless. Ben Parker was liked by all. They passed the main lounge where Mary LeRoy was taking tea with some of her lady friends and moved to one of the side bars.

"Have you heard the latest, Ben?" Hendrik said as their beers were poured.

"No, tell me. Have you decided to shoot the mayor?"

"That's uncanny! Somebody *did* take a potshot at LeRoy! That's what I wanted to tell you!"

Ben gulped back into his beer.

"Wow! Was it you? Was it one of your guns?"

"No, it wasn't me, stupid. Nor one of my guns. At least I don't think so."

"Well, it wasn't me either," said Ben. "Perhaps it was Domino—he was just moaning about the mayor although he seemed pretty relaxed in himself a moment ago. There are plenty of candidates, aren't there? What happened?"

"All I know is that LeRoy was out walking on his own. Mangas wasn't with him for some reason. He was down by the river, way beyond the station, otherwise you would have known, I expect. In the buffer zone. A gun was fired in his direction. He wasn't hit. That's all I know."

"And his wife is having tea over there as calm as you like! Perhaps she fired the gun. You never know!"

"She wouldn't have needed to follow him to the river though, would she?"

"Hendrik, I was only joking! Well, well, the mayor had better watch out!"

Mrs Mary LeRoy was sipping her tea with her friends 'as calm as you like' because she had not heard about somebody shooting at her husband. The incident had happened late last night and whilst news of this type travels fast in some quarters it didn't seem to engage other sections of Nosinalan society quite so quickly. Besides, Mary LeRoy and her friends were actively engaged with the guest they had invited to join them. Mary's society friends had instigated a new pastime which was to invite out to tea the various people profiled each month in the *Nosinalan News*. They had already entertained—or been entertained—by Perry Northrop and the colonel. They might have started their new game because they really wanted to have tea with the governor but the newspaper had not yet profiled him, and in any case, they were nothing if not open to new experiences.

It would be easy to categorise them as prim and proper ladies whose delicacy of constitution and sensibility would never admit anything odorous to assail their senses but there was really nobody like that round these parts. Everybody 'had history' even if some wanted to erase the past. But the 'ladies' didn't even want to do that. They simply enjoyed living their lives in compartments and one of them happened to be afternoon tea in the refined atrium of *The Elgin* which Miles McKay had so tastefully created. So, when Miss Agnes Benson was profiled, they might have thought at first that they had been thrown a wide one but as they considered the unconventionality of having tea with the 85-year-old Agnes who still liked having sex they rather enjoyed the prospect. As it happens, their guest of the moment was far more interesting than their previous 'worthies' so they invited Miss Benson to join them on all their subsequent jollies. Mind you, they still looked forward to tea with Warren Clay, the governor.

Ruby Stevens was all over the news of the shooting at her desk, trying hard to refrain from sensationalism without holding back from the import. Her handling of the news would make it public enough when she published but Hendrik and various others always seemed to be amongst the first to know stuff like this. Not that Ruby was especially bothered on a personal front—it was just another incident when a gun had gone off, although the fact that the mayor was involved added an extra spice, she conceded. Better news, she thought, would have been if the mayor had done the shooting. She was more excited by the profile of Chief Angel who had been selected for the next article. She wanted to interview him herself but felt she should give way to James Blackeagle who had done so well with the Miss Benson piece. On the other hand, she would, perhaps, hold fire on that decision. Pulling rank was a prerogative she had earned.

Hendrik looked across the way at the ladies in deep conversation and laughter in the central court of the hotel and resisted the urge to tell Mrs LeRoy about her husband being shot so the two men fell to talking about other things nothing to do with the mayor or even Nosinala. Hendrik wanted to talk about 'the old country' and Ben was happy to oblige.

It comes to something, you would think when a person being shot at was not overly surprised. It wasn't a case of Frank LeRoy thinking to himself, *What do you expect, you silly bugger, walking down by the river alone?* Plenty of people do that and walk away unscathed. The people of power, those in high places, were perhaps 'fair targets', at times, for the poor and dispossessed, especially if grudges were clung on to in those disparate, desperate places. But the mayor of Nosinala, in the person of Frank LeRoy, seemed to carry a banner round with him which said, "Shoot me if you want. I am to blame." Perhaps that was because his signature was on every piece of paper hated by many. The mayor was to blame for the inequalities of life. For the fact that the no-hoper couldn't get a job. And for the fact that a different low-life couldn't get a girl. It was his fault that the river flooded. And his fault when the river ran dry. He was to blame when the crops failed. When people died. And, probably, from Hendrik's point of view, when people didn't die.

It took a little leap of empathy on his part to realise that it wasn't Frank LeRoy who was hated so much; it was the mayor. Yet he still felt he had a role to play in the betterment of life for those who lived it in and around Nosinala. Mary, his wife, could see why he stayed; Dolly, his mistress, only wanted him to leave. If he had been stronger—or weaker—he would have left Nosinala far behind. But he was neither so he did what all vacillators do and he did nothing. And that included staying to be shot at.

Some men would have said to their best friend, "It goes with the territory."

Frank said to Mangas, "Will you be my bodyguard?"

Some friends would have said, "Let's just get out of here!"

Mangas simply said, "Yes."

At one of the board meetings, some months ago, when Warren Clay had been present in person, the governor asked the meeting, under AOB, of course, "Why do we pay the wages of somebody called Mangas? Who is he?"

The chairperson of the time—Miles McKay—explained he was the personal assistant of the mayor. The colonel added his forthright explanation, "He's a bodyguard."

"But didn't he come with you, Frank, from the mountains?" Jack Bonneville, who liked to drive a point home, asked.

Frank drew a breath.

"Actually, he's from the south."

"You mean he's a Noz?" Jack persisted.

"No, I didn't say that. He is the great-great-grandson of a tribal chief named Black Star."

The governor remained silent.

He's a tribesman dressed in Noz clothing, he thought. He felt even less happy about paying his wages. Though his head was exploding with exclamation marks, the governor decided there was a better way of resolving this matter than in the minutes of a scheduled meeting.

Mangas felt bad that he had not been there for Frank when the bullet had been fired but as Frank had said to him when they were talking about it afterwards, he would not have been able to stop a bullet even if it had been better aimed. Frank's employment of his friend had more to do with the everyday message that his presence sent to those who would otherwise jostle or antagonise at the various public meetings he had to attend. Mangas was a big man but also a man who could calm things down.

"This was not a pre-meditated attack, Mangas. Nobody could have known I was out walking at that time. It wasn't even a good shot. It was a random event. The shooter might not even have known it was me. Just some kid, I expect. I'll tighten up the gun laws. Make possession a little tougher. And I'll round up a few stray rogues just to send out a message. Folk need protecting, I can see that."

Hendrik would not like more restrictions on ownership of guns but he was the least of his problems. Frank would ask the marshals to come down heavy on a few miscreants. That was what they did best.

Marshal Canton got a posse of assistants together and they raided the buffer zone south of the river. Sheriff Nail was not happy at their heavy-handed incursion into 'his' territory, nor with the fact that this northern gang of so-called lawmen—some dozen strong—created local mayhem in one of the run-down bars where aliens were known to congregate. Slapping people around and confiscating weapons, drugs and money was not the best way to keep the peace in Nail's experience especially since it would be left to him to pick up the pieces.

Technically, Sheriff Nail was junior in office to the marshal from the north of the river but it was an uneasy relationship and Marshal Canton never felt confident enough to test the strength of that hierarchical line of command. Nail fumed at yet another mishandling emanating from the mayor's office. Nor was the sheriff the only dangerous man south of the Niba to be left angry.

One of the youths who was badly beaten up by the marshal's men in that raid was the son of a powerful chief of the Conchilla tribe whose name was Red. When Red's son, Rondo, was brought back to the outlying camp of the Conchillas he could barely see out of one eye, his arm had been broken, as well as a few ribs. He had been humiliated and spat on by the marshals from the north. And this was how Red felt too. It was all he could do to control his young bucks who wanted to effect instant revenge. Red managed to show enough measured leadership to restrain his warriors but he also gave full rein to his personal anger when talking to Chief Angel Enrique Cortes about the incident.

"This is more than about one of the Conchillas," he said when the two great leaders met. "This is more than about my son. Rondo needs to learn how to run like a man; now he has the chance as he recovers. But these fights are not of our making. We are being sucked into their petty squabbles. We must do something, Angel."

Red was a long-standing chief in his own right but he respected the almost feudal system of honour accorded to the great Chief Angel. He didn't seek permission to enact his own retribution but he was prepared to make his intentions known before taking any such action. He would have welcomed strategic advice, as well as the not-inconsiderable support of Angel's Esperillos. Red was becoming exasperated by the oscillating revenge attacks that seemed to have characterised their existence over the past few years. The northern Nosinalans would enforce their laws with overt aggression; the Noz would respond in like manner. The Buffer Boys would get involved. Sometimes, renegades from the tribes would be on the periphery. The collateral damage had far-reaching effects.

Angel knew all this. He thought Red was probably right to want action and he was glad he had come to him to talk. Angel thought silently for a while.

"Thank you, my friend. I am sorry for your son and the harm that has been done to him. I am sorry for your shame. You have been insulted. There must be a consequence. But you know that these problems are our problems. Things can't go on as they are. This is bigger than your son."

The two men literally chewed things over whilst sharing food and drink. They talked about their tribes and the conflicts men experienced in living together. They parted in friendship having agreed on a course of action.

The next morning, Deputy Marshal Pointmoor came panting into the mayor's office having run from the river to the market stalls where he commandeered Domino's motorbike which didn't best please Domino.

Pointmoor burst through the door to Frank's office.

"Mayor LeRoy! Mayor! Mangas! Come quick! The river! Hundreds of them! Bloody Hell! Come on!"

Frank came out from his back study and looked at Mangas for some kind of clue as to what was going on.

"Woah, slow down, Pointless! What's troubling you this morning?"

"It's not me! It's them! The tribes! They want you!" He pointed in the direction of the Niba as if those waters would now pour through the door. "Come on!"

Frank thought there was nothing more to be gained by interrogating the deputy marshal further so he put on his waistcoat—for appearances' sake rather than warmth since it was stifling outside even at this early hour of the day. Mangas fixed a shoulder holster under his armpit and eased a second loose shirt over his torso whilst also picking up a rifle that stood against the door. They jumped into their car and left Pointless chewing dust on Domino's stolen bike in their wake.

The main 9.00 o'clock train for the city was waiting to leave from Platform One and there were many dozen—perhaps as many as a hundred—Nosinalans ready to board. The sun gleamed on the red-ochre railings and dogs barked in the distance. The market-traders had already set up their stalls and were doing a brisk business. Domino had watched his bike return under the sweaty thighs of the deputy marshal and he pointed two fingers, in the shape of a trigger, and blew the bastard away. He walked towards the river to reclaim, blame and shame. The bastard! Casual strolling tourists had also gathered towards the riverbank, aware of something else gathering over the Niba. Ben Parker, uncharacteristically, put a stop to the departure of the 9.00 o'clock—he had never seen anything like it.

Sheriff Nail, to the south, emerging from his shack where he had enjoyed a night with a local girl of his favour, took off his hat, spat tobacco on the ground and said, to nobody in particular, "Looks like this'll be an interesting day."

Frank LeRoy arrived with Mangas at his side and took an involuntary gulp as he gazed across the river at the sight that all could behold.

Pointless had under-estimated.

There were well over a thousand tribesmen—and some women—dressed in full warrior regalia, sitting on horses, astride quad bikes, in beaten-up vans, even inside an open-top double-decker bus and standing their ground proud like perennial plants growing from the riverbank. The sound was that of silence save for the occasional snort of a horse, the rev of an engine or the faint barking of dogs. Chief Angel Enrique Cortes sat astride a magnificent white stallion—which, itself, was decked out in colourful feathers, beads and a rich tapestried blanket hanging luxuriously over its flanks—in the centre of the throng.

The stand-off didn't seem fair. For once, those from the south had the upper hand.

Mayor Frank LeRoy was digging deep into inner resources he didn't know he had. This was clearly not a time to flex muscles. All the muscles rippled on the other side. Mangas sucked in a quiet and deep intake of breath and for a moment felt a tug on his soul from the south of the Niba. The river stilled and the air rose into a pregnant pause. It was like the painting of a dream.

Frank LeRoy was nothing if not heroic.

He walked into the river. He knew the right way to walk. He held his hands slightly above his head in a gesture of peace—what other gesture was there in the circumstances?—and he strode slowly forward with a measured deliberation that would have spawned epic poetry in other ages. The ribbon of the bank he had chosen ran unerringly through the swirling waters on either side so that the Niba never rose above his waist at any point. Mangas followed him a few metres behind, his rifle held above his head.

Chief Angel Enrique Cortes watched from the other side. He nodded to Red who was standing poised alongside. Angel dismounted. They advanced slowly into the river to meet the mayor and Mangas in the middle. A Waspero, Autumn Cork by name, joined them in all her six-foot-in-her-boots splendour, her long black hair back-combed, with sharp green eyes blazing and a thick chamois belt around her waist containing a pistol and a hunting knife.

The two groups met in the middle.

"So you are the mayor that everybody wants to kill?" The chief said.

"And you are the chief that everybody loves," replied the mayor.

"So much talk of love and hate, Mr Mayor."

"We are getting this wrong, aren't we?" The mayor said. "And yet here we are, standing as men in the middle of the Wanageeniba, talking. This can go one of two ways," he said.

Frank actually thought this could have gone one of about ten different ways but the same sense that told him to use the full, ancient name of the river also impressed upon him the need to keep things binary. He was thinking of the chief, as well as the colonel, Hank Starling and his agents who had, by now, also congregated in their dozens by the depot. Frank knew that hundreds more would be galvanised with their guns and their prejudices to be sworn in as 'Special Agents'.

"We can talk and agree like men, who have iron and purpose in their souls, or we can fight like cats who walk alone."

Later, Frank came to think that that had been one of his better invented idioms but the urgency of the moment prevented any such fond indulgences.

Angel, with his bloodied feathers and his belt hanging low, with the ringing in his ears of the glorified spirits of the past and his warriors strutting vaingloriously on the southern banks, leant towards Red's ear and they whispered for a while.

Mangas had lowered his rifle in readiness in a kind of poetic movement that sanctified the moment.

Chief Angel returned to the parley.

"Mr Mayor, we are men of the same order. We are diamonds and rust, you and I. But I do not know why men want to kill you. Perhaps we may be granted a time to talk about that. For our part, we wanted to make a point. To make a stance. What happened last night was a tooth for a tooth."

Red bristled a little and Mangas froze.

"But that is over. It is finished. We can settle this now and forever, Mr Mayor, if we are truly men of honour and if we can truly control our factions. In days gone by, we would now cut our hands and grasp them together, you and I, in an understanding. But we are supposed to be civilised. Those days are gone. Shall we just shake hands like the modern man? It is your call, my friend."

The mayor took out a knife and slashed a slice through the open palm of his right hand.

"You've got to cross some rivers before you can call yourself a man, haven't you? Let's do it from my blood to your blood. Our ancestors would recognise the gesture. And let's shake hands in the sight of our people so they might always remember—if they are tempted to stray—that you and I made a covenant, once, here and now."

Chief Angel's eyes sparkled and he freely took the hunting knife offered by the Waspero standing beside him. She looked defiantly at the men opposite her and Mangas lowered his rifle. Angel cut his own hand and the blood ran free, dripping into the Niba.

The mayor and the chief clasped hands without further ceremony and they turned away from each other as if they had been discussing the weather.

The tribes dispersed like passing clouds and the mayor went back to his own people with just a slight pang that he wasn't going back with Angel and the tribes.

Mangas whispered to Frank as they walked back to the bank on the northern side, "Well done, Frank."

The mayor replied, "I was petrified! What about you?"

Mangas thought for a moment.

"That Waspero scared the banshees out of me."

But he was strangely attracted to her too.

It turned out that a raiding band of warriors from Red's Conchillas had, the night before, run amok in a Nosinalan hamlet close to the river just beyond the railway depot and had stolen horses and goods after having beaten up the menfolk who resisted. They were under instructions to kill nobody. Their foray north of the Niba was all about making a threat. Their local chiefs had told the warriors that there was a bigger strategy at work. The band warrior leading the attack couldn't resist the temptation of driving the point home so he chose the strongest young man he could find amongst those homesteaders, dragged him down to the river by attaching ropes to his stallion, cut off his eyebrows, broke his ribs and buried him up to his neck in sand, not caring whether the Niba would flood or not.

The boy was found some hours later a gibbering wreck.

Chief Angel Enrique Cortes wanted to make the point that his tribesmen and women could do so much more damage if they wanted. That was why they turned out in such silent force the next day. Angel knew that north of the Niba there existed many more men than his tribes could ever contemplate and that they would just continue to pour in to affect their own retribution whenever they wanted but he knew, also, that there were amongst such men leaders, visionaries, powerful voices who would want to see a peaceful resolution. He knew that the terms of peace were written out on treaties that blew in the wind but he also clung on to the hope that sometimes a man's word could be trusted from whatever side of the river he had been born. That was why he had persuaded Red to let him speak with the mayor.

Angel's terms were fair and they could be conceded by the northern Nosinalans without loss of face. And Red and his warlike kinsmen could see the value of the future.

Angel proposed to Frank LeRoy that a line was drawn under the beatings of Rondo and the lad by the depot. And furthermore, the tribes would be given a ten-year chance to take control of all new and existing casinos south of the river. There would be no interference or obstacles from the north. If they couldn't make things work, they would cease all activity and pass back rights to the north. Angel didn't particularly like gambling, as a livelihood, but he liked the drug trade so much less and it was those drugs that were beginning to attract the interests of his young men. Angel thought that the casinos could lead to other leisure and tourist opportunities and he was nothing if not pragmatic. In truth, he would have wanted nothing better than to travel further south, find a new river and hunt and fish there for the rest of his days but he recognised that he was part of the old order and that times had moved on. The casinos seemed to be a useful bargaining chip.

Frank thought that a concession of this kind would be easy to drive home with the board of members—who never really cared much for the south anyway (apart from the access to the minerals which they had pretty well sewn up already)—especially if people like Miles McKay could continue to expand their operations to the north. Plus, he reasoned, the members of the board didn't have one thousand native warriors armed to the teeth bristling within view when the proposal was laid out in the middle of the gentle waters of the Niba. That was the gist of the conversation between Chief Angel Enrique Cortes and Mayor Frank LeRoy whose hunter and warrior instincts had been reduced—or elevated—to the power of words in the shallows of the Niba on that stilled and sunlit morning when the northern city train and the southern desert horses snorted.

At the very moment that Frank LeRoy was wading into the Niba to confront Chief Angel Enrique Cortes, two women intimately tied to him met, by chance, some five miles north of the river in a place called Coppertown. It was a small settlement that had developed some chic boutiques and tourist venues alongside the faded mining history it had once boasted when it was first founded as 'Coppertown'. Frank had been engaged early that morning with his own assignment in the middle of the river 'where true waters and true men meet', so the saying went, and it had been even earlier for Mary LeRoy and Dolores Bellworthy. The ladies had not planned to meet it has to be said. They kept apart from each other in Nosinala so they were hardly likely to co-ordinate their diaries in quirky little Coppertown.

But it is passing strange, is it not, that when great moments of potential import occur in their own place and their own time, almost as if they had been pre-destined, according to whim or the movement of the spheres or the will of the gods, there often also happens events of possibly lesser consequence in some other place at the same time?

The mayor's wife had arranged to see a delegation of liberal society ladies who were anxious about the rough edges of the Nosinalan territories below them on the map. They thought that the mayor's wife might be able to understand and support them in their wish to keep their lives 'clean'. The mayor's mistress had made the journey north to meet an old friend who wanted to make urgent contact.

After Mary LeRoy had heard out the ladies she was meeting, who were dressed in very fine clothes which complemented perfectly their very fine noses, she considered her response. They had been twittering like birds, hopping around the arid gardens of their lives, preening themselves, squawking, jabbing their silly beaks into the business of others because they had no business worth talking about of their own.

"What do you think, Mrs LeRoy?"

"Let me get this right. You are objecting to the presence of *The Sunrise Parlour* in our little town, is that right? You don't like the fact that there are prostitutes at work behind closed doors. And you don't like it that the reverend shakes hands with *that* woman. You don't like the way she walks up and down the High Street smiling and nodding to some of the men. Have I got that about right?"

At the mention of the word 'prostitute', the ladies sitting opposite had to put down their tea cups.

"Yes, Mrs LeRoy, that's it!"

"Well, look, ladies. Have you considered what would happen to those girls who Molly Doyle looks after if things were otherwise? They would be on the streets after dark. They would be much more vulnerable. Last week, I heard that one young lady had stopped working at *The Sunrise* having made enough money to move upstate and is now running a corner shop. Isn't that good?"

"They're hardly young *ladies*!"

Mary LeRoy let that pass. She continued, "And what about the men and their needs? Do you ever wonder whether Molly Doyle smiles, in recognition, at your husbands when they pass her by in town?"

"Mrs LeRoy! Whatever do you mean? My Henry would have nothing to do with that dreadful woman!"

"Why don't you ask your husbands if they would be as keen as you are to shut down *The Sunrise Parlour*?"

Mary's lips formed a thin smile for she was beginning to tire of all this civilised outrage. She stood up and said, "Better still, why don't you all fuck off?"

Clearly, she had the upper hand at this point and she sailed out of the tea-rooms with a suitably regal air.

Dolores Bellworthy had just dismissed her male friend with a similar riposte, in sentiment, if not by force of language. He had suggested to her that 'there was living space in the east'. They could start again. Pick up where they had left off.

"Michael, much as I admire you, love you, I cannot. This is not the time nor the place. You should have asked me a year ago. Or perhaps in a few months' time. Who knows? Oh, why don't you just go?!"

Mary strode off down the boardwalk like a galleon in full sail, wishing she had met people in places where different winds blew; Dolores shimmered translucently with a whiff of regret, wondering if she had boarded the wrong vessel on the waters she travelled.

They met, these two surging brigantines, under the glare of the ripening sun.

"Now this would be Mrs Bellworthy, I presume, the *lady* from the south," said Mary.

Dolores couldn't fail to pick up the intonation of the word 'lady'.

She gathered herself.

"And you must be Mary, the wife of the mayor."

They knew each other, of course, but the rituals and the drama were important.

They encountered a stand-off of their own.

"Shall we sit for a while in the shade of the trees?" Dolly said. "We could watch the children playing or we could drink or we could talk."

"Let's do all three," said Mary, "But I insist on paying."

"Alright, but why don't you call me Dolly?"

"Because he calls you that. And you may continue to call me Mrs LeRoy."

"Mary! Don't be poncey! It's Christian name terms for thee and me or it is nothing."

The mayor's wife looked at the woman standing in front of her.

"Ok, I'll call you Dolly to your face."

Dolores smiled.

"It's a start," she said. And she took Mary by the arm and led her to some seats under a tree, making sure she ordered a bottle of white wine from the waiter at the nearby outside bar.

What is it that two women who share the same man talk about when they are sitting together under a tree? Everything, it seems, except the man. They spent an hour there for all the world like sisters. Frank would not have liked it if they had been talking about him and might have been slightly put out that they did not. But there was no blood which must count for something.

Later, with the benefit of perspective, Mary LeRoy looked back on that hour with Dolly and realised she had been fuming inside the whole time. She marvelled at her ability to retain such gracious civility on the outside whilst harbouring such thoughts of evil intent within. Perhaps it had been the same for the woman called Dolores Bellworthy. Mary hated her. She hated the fact of her. She would kill her and that would exorcise the ghost. No, she would kill Frank. It became a stimulating game she played in her head. 'How to Kill Frank' could have become a good working title for a novel. It became another ghost that lived in her head.

And so the ghosts enter the story.

Mary LeRoy was not the only person to carry around with her ghosts of her own making. Frank had ghosts, dreams if you like, of somebody trying to kill him. Mind you, there were times when somebody really did seem to try to kill him so perhaps they weren't really ghosts at all in any conventional kind of sense. Mangas knew all about the river ghosts and the ghosts of the mountain since he had felt them. Dolly was escaping ghosts from her past; Sheriff Nail lived with ghosts every day, as did many who drew their living from the river and the border lands on either side.

They knew that the ghosts lived in the wind-that-whispers, the *Skanze*, that blew up from nowhere and settled back down again on a whim. The tribespeople further south danced with the cloud ghosts in commemoration of ancient ceremonies and the jackals fed off the ghosts hallucinated by their drug-addict victims whose lives writhed and intertwined in the dirt-tracks and the dust. Even Reverend Hopkins prayed to ghosts that his religion had invented investing the Holy Ghost with a veneer of sacramentality that was supposed to be so much more respectable than the pagan spirits given due accord elsewhere. Some people were frightened of the ghosts of Nosinala; others embraced them like old friends; still more leant on them as crutches without which they could not go on. Digger Brown paid them no heed though he and his miners saw things best left undisturbed underground.

And then there were the ghosts in Saddles Boarding House.

Henry and Olive Saddles had run the old boarding house as long as anybody could remember and the house itself had fallen down, been rebuilt and was now extended to four-storeys on a plot on the edge of town. It was as if Nosinala had grown around it and then beyond it, embarrassed perhaps by its fading grandeur, its link with the past. Saddles had been a watering hole, a brothel, some say even a chapel, but its primary purpose these days was to offer up its twelve rooms to weary or excited travellers. Henry and Olive lived very happily in a small bungalow at the bottom of the garden that led back to the house. From there, they could arrive through the kitchen door at about 6.00 am and start to prepare the breakfasts. Through the door of the Residents' Lounge, they would retire about midnight back into the garden and onto the path that would take them the twenty-five metres to their own dwelling once more. The ghosts at Saddles were inconveniencing at first and business definitely suffered.

People didn't want to feel uneasy in their beds. But, as is sometimes the way with strange phenomena, a counter-culture grew, almost a cultish interest, so that Henry and Olive came to realise that the ghosts were their greatest assets. People came from far and wide to stay at Saddles. Guests would even ask for a particular room if they thought it was lived in or visited by one of the Saddles' ghosts. It was probably one of the few places of hospitality where it was not seen as a problem to guests when booking if a room was 'already occupied'.

Any statement from Henry saying 'Sorry, that room is taken' might be received with delight. Guests would experience sensations as they moved about the house. The air would become colder even on the hottest of days and then return to its normal temperature. Pictures would come crashing down off walls, objects would fall from tables, footsteps could be heard in empty rooms and corridors on floors above and the fame of Saddles spread. Olive privately blamed her husband's useless skills at fixing paintings or she would know it was the uneven table surfaces or the great age of the creaking floorboards simply moaning and groaning with the burden of holding up the house but the guests thought otherwise.

Plus, of course, there were the apparitions. There was *The Lady Who Screamed*—the prostitute murdered in her bed many years before. There was *Billy the Boy Ghost* who just liked to mess about or sometimes sit under the tables when the guests were eating. And there was also *The Old Gardener* who pottered about in the back yard late at night softly whistling his tunes that kept his plants and his dreams alive all these years later. To see or smell one of the ghosts became a trendy pastime. Henry and Olive did nothing to disabuse their guests of the notion that 'here be spirits' of the past.

"Hello, Mr Saddles," would go the refrain, "Any activity likely tonight, d'ye think?"

Henry Saddles always had a conspiratorial look about him as he usually lowered his voice to pass on a whispered confidentiality, "Not for me, nor Mrs Saddles, to say, my friend. But if we all stay alert, you never know!"

There were only six paying guests at Straddles at this time: Peter and Polly Horner—with their pretty fifteen-year-old daughter, Eve; a newly-married couple from the west—Zac and Cheyenne Wallace—who were on a touring holiday; and Robson Calhoun, a writer. The Horners were assessing the value of the locale as a suitable place to re-settle; they paid no attention to the rumours of ghosts, for they had no time for such nonsense, which was out of kilter with Eve since she spent a lot of time in the empty rooms above them looking for *The Boy Billy* and on more than one occasion had entered into conversation with *The Old Gardener*. Zac and Cheyenne had booked a room at Saddles with the deliberate intention of confronting a ghost story or two to tell their friends back home and Robson Calhoun was always looking for good copy to write about. Calhoun, in fact, looked like a ghost himself with his sleek prematurely white hair and his sallow complexion. He walked silently around the boarding house and once made even Olive Saddles jump when he appeared as if from nowhere, on the landing of the second floor.

"Oh, Mr Calhoun! You gave me such a fright!" she said.

"I'm sorry, Mrs Saddles. I think I'm on the wrong floor. Too busy thinking, I expect. I didn't mean to startle you."

"You're fine, you're fine," she said, brushing a fleck of dust from her shoulder, "But your room is on the first floor. That's why it's called 301."

Calhoun looked a little quizzical as if about to question her further, but he simply said, "You're right. It's 301. I've gone up another flight of stairs. So sorry."

Olive had never really understood why her husband had not just numbered their twelve rooms from 1 to 12. That would have been the sensible thing to do. But Henry had some grand idea that the first floor would house rooms 301, 302, 303 and 304, with the second floor accommodating the first four 200s, and the third floor taking care of the four 100s. She thought he had copied it from some swanky hotel they had once stayed in many years ago but she hadn't been sure. Maybe he was just being deliberately quirky—as if their boarding house needed any more oddness!

She had always said that the guests would become confused. Besides, whatever the number on the door, some rooms always remained 'Billy's Room' or 'The Sad-eyed Lady's Room' according to whoever was passing through. But whatever the case turned out to be, and despite all pretensions to the contrary, nobody really remained the same after spending a few nights in Room 101 at the top. Olive liked the fact that their ghosts—if they had any—were benign but she didn't enjoy going into Room 101 herself when there was cleaning and there was airing to be done. It was the only room in the house where she felt unwelcome. And notwithstanding her numerous attempts to scour the floorboards and wash the walls, she could not eradicate the slightly foul smell that gathered when the door was closed. She always left the window there wide open. Some guests complained of the cold at night but they usually had a different complaint the next morning when they shut the window tight. Except they rarely found the courage or the words to explain the nature of their complaint. The usual pattern for guests of Room 101 was to pay the bill hurriedly and move on. Henry Saddles thought she was just being 'fond' as he called it.

"There's nothing wrong with Room 101!" he'd say. "Why don't we sleep there ourselves one night? Then you'd see!"

"Why don't you sleep there, Henry, on your own? Then we'll see if you check out the next morning!"

But Henry never did sleep there on his own.

The stories grew. Ruby Stevens even ran an article called Room 101 in the *Nosinalan News* and though Olive wished it had never been written, Henry thought it was good for business.

In any event, Robson Calhoun was in Room 301. On the first floor. The three Horners had two adjoining rooms on the second floor. And Zac and Cheyenne enjoyed the privacy of the top floor in Room 104.

Henry and Olive Saddles padded back and forth, back and forth, from their cosy dwelling at the far end of the garden, tied into their routines like worker bees, gathering honey, even if Henry's role—as a drone—had long since transmogrified into that of a worker, too. Henry and Olive had never been blessed with children so perhaps he had never been a drone anyway.

But ghosts come and go, do they not, even if they ever appear in the first place? Real life happened in the here and now with the living, where controls could be put in place.

And the control of events fell to some to administer in a way that was not the case for others to whom and for whom the administering was delivered, sometimes altruistically, but more often than not, with a tint of less than benign dictatorship.

Frank LeRoy had encountered, by chance, Perry Northrop in the centre of town not long after the shooting. Northrop was concerned that the aliens were still about. It's almost out of control—it's not good for business, he had said. Frank said it wasn't good for his health either but that point didn't seem to drive home.

"Anyway," said Frank, "I need to add an agenda point for our next meeting. Chief Angel Enrique Cortes has a proposition that is interesting and which might resolve a lot of our problems. He is a good man, you know. Honest and truthful, I think."

Northrop looked at Frank askance.

"The board will decide what is truthful," he said.

Frank laughed but realised quickly that Perry Northrop wasn't joking.

When Mary and Dolly had made their way back to Nosinala following their emotionally charged accidental meeting under the trees in Coppertown, they both found out about Frank being shot at and immediately showed more personal concern for him than that which Perry Northrop had expressed.

Dolly, particularly, was upset. She sent so many messages to Frank but could not get through to him and he did not reply. She was strangely knocked out of her stride by his silence so she did something she had never done before: she drove to his house in the hope of seeing him privately, just to find out if he was safe. She drew up in the wide road opposite Frank's house where he lived with Mary and Bobby. It was early evening and the light was beginning to fade. She could see figures moving about through the large window at the front of the house and then saw Frank step out onto the porch for a smoke.

She phoned him instantly. She watched him reach for his phone and she knew he would know it was her calling. Her name would come up on his phone. Or at least the name she used when she phoned him. She was down in his phone list as 'Office'. They both thought that would be more discreet. She saw him read the phone name and then ignore it. She felt he had slapped her in the face. Perhaps she was wrong to go to his house. She had made things awkward. Frank would be angry. She saw him go back into the house and Mary came up to him and kissed him. He kissed her in return. They sat down on a sofa close together and she saw them raise a glass to each other. What was happening? This was not how Frank had described their domestic lives. Mary then came to the window and pulled the curtain strings. She looked out and Dolly sank lower in her car. She did not think she had been seen. The curtains drew closed and Dolly sped off with her eyes smarting and her mind whirling.

Mary sat down next to her husband and said, "I'm so glad you're alright. But I worry about you. It's this kind of thing that reminds us what's important, don't you agree? We should do this more often, Frank."

But Frank was thinking of Dolly. He knew he had to provide for his wife and for Bobby but he wished he was at Cavendish Avenue.

Dolly drove round for a bit and then went home. She couldn't make sense of things. She kept on coming up with rational explanations for his reason not to answer her messages and his reason for not speaking on the phone. And perhaps the kiss was just a familiar peck on the cheek. And what was wrong with that? They were married after all. But then they sat together so intimately! But that was what chairs were for—sitting on. *This is stupid*, she thought. *I'll have to see him. No, I'll just go silent and see whether he bothers to come to me.*

She thought of her meeting with Mary who wanted Dolly to call her 'Mrs LeRoy'. And then a text pinged in. It would be Frank! But it was not Frank; it was Michael Stead, her first love whom she had met up with again in Coppertown. He had come back onto the scene and had wanted her to go with him back to the east—though she had declined despite knowing that first love runs deep. Michael's text said, 'Dolly, it was good to meet. The offer's still open.' Life had become more complicated.

Reverend William Hopkins had just begun his sermon.

"Today, I want to talk to you about the South American sword-billed hummingbird and the way the wind blows when it's angry…"

He liked to get the attention of his congregation with what he thought were provoking images but, in reality, it didn't much matter what he said or how he put it because the church-goers were all regulars and they either fell asleep, regardless, or they listened intently, equally regardless of the content of the homily. Listening—or not listening—was simply signified by eyes open or shut and nobody could tell who was doing what. The reverend pressed on. He wrote his homilies down and sent them to parishioners who might not have been able to attend that week (it was remarkable how many townsfolk were otherwise engaged when there was a service) and, in any case, he hoped that the bishop might come to read one of his sermons and comment favourably. The bishop, way upstate, might have commented had he had his own eyes open but he seemed to slumber even more than the parishioners.

Winnie Crane was one of the locals who sat devotedly looking up at William. She had grown ever closer to the reverend and enjoyed their regular meetings when they discussed social matters and the environment in which all the townspeople lived. She took her responsibilities seriously as a member of the board. Winnie thought, initially, that the input and endorsement from the local churchman would be an important 'rubber-stamping' of her efforts to improve the lives of others, especially the downtrodden.

"There are so many poor souls who are lost, don't you agree, William?"

"That is certainly true. But, do you know, those souls lose more than themselves when they come to church? I keep a Lost Property section in the back cupboards. I record the details in the parish newsletter. I announce things lost at the pulpit sometimes. But nobody ever comes forward to claim them."

"What sort of things do people leave behind?"

"You won't believe me when I tell you! Oh, there are hats and gloves and spectacles, of course, but I found two sets of false teeth on one of the pews one week! Then there was the lost child."

"How could somebody lose a child at church?" Winnie asked laughing.

"I won't tell you her name but Mrs So-and-So came to church with her son—let's call him Johnny—and she shook my hand to say goodbye at the end of the service and went off home. I saw off all the other members of the congregation and locked the church. An hour later, I heard some knocking from inside the church doors. I was tending to the garden strips outside. I opened up the church and there was Johnny! He had been mostly sitting on one of the pews staring up at the crucifix—probably too frightened to move, I expect—thinking that his mother would be back for him soon. When I walked him home his mother had not noticed he was missing! Are these the lost souls you are talking about, Winnie?"

They were both laughing now and the more Winnie met William to discuss the town, the more she realised that what she really wanted to do was discuss the two of them. It came to her one day after a particularly successful encounter when they had covered a great deal of business and she had felt validated in what she was doing with her life. William made her feel that way. He approved of her. She enjoyed his company. She always came away with a warm glow of satisfaction in her breast until she realised with a flush to her face that she wasn't just thinking about the poor of Nosinala.

It was about this time that Molly Doyle finally took up William's jocular invitation to come to church. He had said 'there was always a place at the front', hadn't he? The

Sunshine Parlour was still her life—she wasn't about to embrace a Damascene moment—but there might have been something missing, that much she would acknowledge. And there was always the soothing voice of the reverend. And his eyes. And his hands. She could dream, couldn't she, whilst other church-goers indulged their own particular fantasies. It would be a poor kind of god that didn't welcome sinners. She took delight in making the worthy Winnie Crane shove along the pew at the front. There were now at least two ladies looking up at William.

A lesser man, or greater, might have been distracted but William felt validated, himself, when he saw Molly Doyle settle down in her Sunday Best. Another soul seeking something that had been lost or perhaps just another lonely person wanting to step out of the eye of the storm. He was never judgemental even if Winnie had created more space than she needed to accommodate the Madam from the *Sunshine Parlour*.

William thought he would throw in a few more colourful metaphors to jostle with the humming bird and the angry wind. He referenced the symmetrical stories carved in stone on the façade of a cathedral. He talked about the featureless sliding face of an iceberg. And he might have drawn out the disjointed, fractured images of a cut-glass diamond, by way of comparison. The architecture of man, nature and God is the same and different. Of course, they could all have been the wrong words in the wrong place but there was just a chance he might have struck home with somebody and that would have made it worthwhile. Wasn't that what people wanted when they came to church? A chance to remove themselves from their realities. And what better way to usher them in than to indulge in the language of metaphor and symbolism?

One of the reasons why Perry Northrop was anxious about the aliens and any unfettered intrusions into the cosier life of Nosinala North was because of the upcoming Lacrosse Festival.

The savages and aliens could be managed in Northrop's heart and mind as long as he thought of them as inhuman. It was when the possibility slunk into his conscious thought that they might be actually human, in the same fullness as he was, that the fall horror of such contemplation was driven home. Imagine if they were just like him! That would imply kinship, responsibility, and fellow-feeling: a bridge too far for Northrop. The tribesmen and women were fine if they stayed in their place. And that was why the Lacrosse Festival worked so well. The natives could be, well, natives, and the Nosinalans and tourists could marvel at the spectacle and then leave it all behind. That was the narrative he chose to believe. It would be better for all concerned if people stuck to their allotted roles.

The Lacrosse Festival was probably the only event in the Nosinalan calendar that brought all people together. It lasted for six days and nights. The nights were as important as the days. It was reckoned that three days would lead to complete and continuous drunkenness but that by extending to six days most participants would have to pace themselves a little, draw in the reins, as it were, down tools and take a breath—however you might like to put it. And it was the drawing of breath that brought the most benefits in the minds of many because that was when all parties encountered the spirits most nearly to themselves. They could breathe. And when people breathe deeply, they find an authenticity which strips away the artifices we like to scaffold about our lives and identities. Not that all the contributors to this festival might articulate it like that but the end result was the same whether they were consciously aware of the phenomenon or not.

'Contributors' turned out to be a far more accurate descriptor than 'participants' because the spectators, the visitors, the young and the old—who might not have been so actively participating in the running and the racing and the mayhem of the lacrosse—were vital component parts of the organism that was the festival. Without them, there would have been no strutting, no ceremonies, no depth of purpose. It is an interesting philosophical question: can anyone achieve local, regional or worldwide fame in the simple enactment of the contest? Or does such conferment only really happen when there are others present to record and applaud and reflect upon the moment? In any event, the Lacrosse Festival—six days long—was about to start and, as for other years, it had its requisite number of participants and contributors to render the debate irrelevant.

To say that the festival energised the local community, or that it attracted people from far and wide, or that it characterised, contrariwise, the coalescence of the place, despite the effluence that would seep excrementally, shall we say, rather than flow incrementally in ways civilised people would prefer, would be an understatement. No wonder God, on the seventh day, rested.

We should say something about lacrosse. It sounds French. It could be 'Lecrosse', could it not, since it is masculine and brutal at its core, but the feminine designation also works, does it not? Besides, it is sometimes called 'Le

Lacrosse' which smacks of hedging one's bets a tad. Let us just say that if you want to play 'lacrosse', you would do well to be male and quick and strong. If you want to play as a female you should be male and quick and strong. And if you don't like the first condition, then you'd better be canny and quick and strong.

There are versions of the game, as it has developed, in Europe and other places, where there are rules. The game that was played on the meadowlands south of the Nosinala Niba had few rules. One rule that had an immediate attraction to the uninitiated was the requirement 'not to headbutt'. To the initiated that was an unnecessary addition to ancient protocols. There were other rules, it should be said. *No choking, no breaking of limbs and no gratuitous grabbing of an opponent's genitalia* were clearly brought in as rules when transgressions of the same apparently occurred regularly although the term 'gratuitous' was still interpreted liberally.

The game was started by the ball toss of a female who had been elected for the task. Sometimes she would simply raise an eyebrow. The players had to watch closely. And the proceedings were adjudicated by the Elders who used to deliberate, and then pronounce, on matters of contention, in between their smoking and drinking of the various crushed leaves and seeds of the plants that grew by the river. Teams would be allowed to field twelve players each, or forty-five, depending on which version of the game was being played. Matches would last until the first goal had been scored or for twenty-four hours and would include the time of night spell when many of the best passages of play occurred (although not everyone could recall the details after the event).

But it wasn't all about the lacrosse.

Around the pitch—which could be an acre or three depending on the floodplain—there developed exponentially, laterally and often intravenously, an organic abundance of parasitic bacchanalia that was not (entirely) fuelled by alcohol, narcotics or spiritual epiphanies induced by hysteria, indulgence and feeble minds. Many of the activities were as pure and virtuous as any puritanical or pious spirits might like to embrace. And if you wanted candyfloss there was candyfloss. It was a veritable carnival!

One of the less feeble minds belonged to Sheriff Nail. He liked the wild ecstasies as long as they didn't incur his wrath. Some celebrations were benign. At one such dance, he was even seen to take off his shirt and shimmy seductively with the others, some of whom were maidens, others oil-skinned youths ardent for some kind of glory. There were other medieval rhythms when the dance became violent and his muscular frame was called upon to separate the fools from the foolhardy. He liked those moments less.

All the hotels were now full. So was Saddles. And some people had taken to camping in makeshift tents on both sides of the river. Storms were forecast but the timing was unpredictable. For the moment, the heat remained oppressive even if clouds gathered as the day wore on. On the weather front, one pattern that could emerge would be for the skies to open overnight only for the sun to return for the daylight hours. Another model could be that when the storm broke it would just rain for three whole days. And yet another scenario would be that the storm would pass them by and dump itself 200 miles downriver. The residents and visitors took no heed; what would be, would be.

But the mayor had his own way of putting it as he said to Mangas, "When the frogs are croaking in the lagoon, the rain will come real soon."

Mangas ignored the weather prediction and hadn't, in any case, heard any frogs croaking, but he was extra-vigilant about his friend's safety following the seemingly random shooting recently.

"Why didn't you call for me, Frank, that night when the gun went off?"

"You know I like to be alone sometimes, especially at night. Anyway, all will be well. Shall we stroll down to the game? Things should be starting soon."

Mangas prepared to leave the mayor's office. He picked up his rifle which was really like another arm and reached up to touch the top of the door frame and this time, the sides of the frame as well. He even did a little jig as he left the office. Frank smiled.

"Come on, old friend, if we're going to fall it might as well be from a donkey as from an ox."

Mangas couldn't see any donkeys or oxen either, as well as not hear the frogs croak. And he was supposed to be the one with intuitive insights in his bones.

Frank had put on his most colourful waistcoat as if he had been asked to start the proceedings with a flourish. But that honour always fell to the old lady. Besides, she could outdo the mayor any day in her resplendent flowing robes that shone like peacock feathers. She was somewhere to be found down by the meadow that was to serve as the playing arena. Frank and Mangas strolled down through the town where business was brisk in the shops and coffee outlets.

Perry Northrop was preening himself somewhere safe and clean, delighted that the festival season had got off to such a bumper start. He was busily involved in a live link with *The Nosinalan News* and only mildly disgruntled that he wasn't deemed important enough to be talking to Ruby Stevens herself. Ruby had traversed the Niba and was tracking down Chief Angel Enrique Cortes who had promised her a one-on-one interview. Hank Starling was bristling, even as Colonel Wesley Harding was brooding moodily, over events that might yet unfold. Miles McKay could hardly keep his hands from joining together, with each other, in a peremptory congratulation about his good fortune and business acumen in buying into the entertainment, accommodation and leisure business.

The bells and the lights of the border-land casinos rang and sang in celebration of good times returned and retained their reputation as one of the few places where prejudice never reigned. The only requirement asked was 'Could you pay your way'? Actually, the best requirement was that you could *not* pay your way. It was then that the hook took hold. Frank LeRoy knew this all too well. It was remarkable how often his private evening walks took him down to the glitter and allure of Casino Land. He had used a good deal of his money from the mountain days and had started to dip into the stake provided by Mangas whose trust was unquestioning. Their joint ventures, though ethically dubious, had produced significant returns and they had invested together in a bank account that yielded high interest as long as a level of capital remained. Mangas handed over happily the management of the account to Frank. Why would he not trust him? Had he not saved his life on those mountain slopes when the snows came down and the hunters had become the hunted? And why would Frank not speculate with his friend's share of their money when the roulette wheel span cruelly or when the cards fell bad? Everything was temporary. The wheel would spin fortuitously again. It was no wonder Frank LeRoy, the mayor, could find himself accommodating the wishes of Chief Angel Enrique Cortes. Any friend in a casino was a friend indeed.

Mangas and Frank continued on their way. They took a tour around the river markets and Domino watched them go thinking that one day he would wear a waistcoat far better than the one sported by the mayor. Business was booming. Dogs barked, children played and Wilson Creek was selling 'authentic' medieval drinking vessels by the dozen (for he kept a plentiful supply of such unique items in the back of the store). The mayor even saw a man walk by with the embalmed head of a crocodile under his arm.

Possibly, the only person disappointed would have been the Reverend William Hopkins in that the values he held dear seemed to be put on hold at these times. Converts only happened when it was raining. He looked up at the skies. There were clouds and stars but not much manna falling, that much he could grant. Perhaps the dewfall would work its magic. Sorry, its miracles. From William's point of view, the only good thing to emerge on a personal front was the fact that he could take off his dog collar. Even a man of the cloth could fashion his own sabbatical, could he not?

And Molly Doyle had already made arguably the more difficult move by sitting in the front pew of his church. He wandered, too, on that gathering day, graciously accepting a drink from an itinerant pedlar whose concoctions were designed to beguile and succumb. God can surely be found in all kinds of places or there is no god at all. And Molly would be wandering, also.

Carson Wong, the inscrutable manager of the most popular casino known as *The Chrysalis*, was standing outside his establishment as Mangas and the mayor strolled by. Carson Wong was far from home except that *this* was now his home. His ancestors hailed from the shimmering back streets of Hong Kong where geomancers from Kowloon shook hands with the snakes found hiding in the New Territories and where practitioners of the ancient art of feng shui joined the entourage of pirate ghosts that tracked his footsteps even here, even now. The eyes had it. Frank LeRoy and Carson Wong dilated in recognition then turned aside to other things. There was an understanding between men that negated further consent. We shall see each other soon, there's no more to be said.

The walk and then the river crossing to the Game of Lacrosse took on a character and pageantry of its own. There were traders bargain-yelling; artisans displaying; oils hissing on deep-pan fryers; exotic dresses spangling; oaths being made and the same oaths squandered; the running and drifting and laughing and shouting of people ecstatic; animals wild and creatures domestic splashing and crashing in territories new; and garrulous gods and ghosts, gracious, mingling without precedence in the river enduring.

The hearts raced, the veins pulsed and the blood banged in the brain.

"Let the game begin!" screeched the old lady with a twitch of her mouth.

There had been a compromise because of the weather that was meant to turn. It would be 24 players per team and the match would be finished 24 hours later unless other circumstances dictated. The Elders were delegated to decide what those other circumstances might entail. The players hardly cared about the parameters of playing time. The pitch was a cow meadow. But the players were shining. There were 800 metres between the posts. The players formed clusters and wrestled each other in pairs off the ball whilst other small groups battled to gain supremacy in other ways through speed, position and strategy. And a few others tried hard to win possession of the ball. They all wielded sticks. Some players had two sticks though it wasn't clear whether that was an advantage or not. The defenders had bigger sticks. And mayhem ensued.

Ruby Stevens couldn't believe her luck. She had expected the chief to invite her to his tent, pitched somewhere further south. But she had not reckoned on the fact that the Esperillos were playing the Conchillas. She had not held out the strongest of hopes that he would be willing or able to grant any kind of interview in the first place but when his representative had contacted her to say he would be happy to talk at the beginning of the game at pitch-side, as it were, she snapped at the chance. She wasn't sure what to expect. She had been told that sometimes the chief communicated simply by pursing his lips. She thought that if that was the case she would have a lot of blanks to fill in for her readers.

"Chief Angel Enrique Cortes—this seems as good a place as any to start since we are sitting here together as witnesses to this grand spectacle. Why is this so important?"

"Because it is The Creator's Game. But you are not sitting, Ruby Stevens. Sit. Smoke this. It will make you see more."

Ruby was not sure she should smoke the burning weed she was offered, nor that she needed to see more, as the chief put it, but she sat, dutifully enough, then thought better of her reticence. Perhaps the aroma had already reached her nostrils.

"I will," she said, "though I'm not expecting to see more."

"Only those who do not see well say that," said Angel.

Ruby inhaled and sat there with the chief in the temporary tepee he had erected near the meadow that had become the lacrosse field of play. And after a while, though she could hear the sound of Angel's voice, she could also hear another soft voice—which was not hers, she didn't think—and once, she seemed to soar above the two of them like a bird looking back down on herself, the game, the people and the river that no longer divided the two Nosinalas but flowed like a central blood vessel. She wanted to swim in the Niba, feel the heat of the sun and the warm waters coalesce in and around her body.

It was perhaps only a moment—or it lasted for an hour—but she returned to her body and she looked at the chief who was watching the game with his eyes closed. They talked about many things. She went away later to write up her interview like no other before but she knew that the article that made the final print of the paper did not capture the experience she had had that day with Angel Enrique Cortes. It was as if she had felt love for the first time, the best time, in a private box at an opera. She was meant to be a pragmatic journalist but somehow, she had become caught up in the intoxication of the moment. She had become humbled, stripped and laid bare. She came to realise that she had been trying to apply her intellect to a task that was rendered emotional. She had been using her brain instead of her spirit. At this place where boundaries were constructed, she had been building metaphysical barriers of her own. Simplicity won the day over sophistication. There was no need to don a cloak to wear as a heavy disguise. All this—and more—the chief had taught her.

One insight the chief had shared with her became the title of her article: *The right to travel one's own path is inalienable.*

And the operatic qualities of the Lacrosse Festival continued through the day and long into the night. The spectacles, the convoluted extremities of lyric and plot, the struggling and subversive passions and the entire soaring stage rendered it a mystifying experience bordering on hallucination and enchantment. The threatened rain did not come. People of all hues interacted and played their parts well according to their dispositions. Sometimes they surpassed themselves. For the most part, harmony was the order of the day. A few minor skirmishes between youths did not mar the overall celebrations. Besides, the game provided enough violence to keep the belligerent engaged.

It wasn't entirely clear to the disinterested spectator but the game was heading into its dark phase with the Conchillas leading by two goals to one. There would be play of a sort through the night but the rules of engagement changed somewhat and the uninitiated would have had even greater difficulty keeping up, as did some of the players, it has to be said. But by daybreak, somebody in authority would know the score and new players would be allowed to join the game whilst the die-hards would continue. Other stalls and activities continued, too, for a while longer, but once dusk settled in properly, most crowds from the day began to find their way back to their homes and their temporary accommodation even as a new breed of reveller was arriving to eat and drink and dance the night away. And the casinos started their business in earnest.

The daytime flutterers had frittered away small-fry stakes and might even had enjoyed the thrill of a minor win but the newly-installed dens and the well-established halls awaited their regular patrons, the serious players, who would arrive with the night. Darkness provided a measure of anonymity when the voices of conscience could not always make themselves heard above the din in the gamblers' heads but it was more than that. Some gambled at night because they had run out of other things to do. Some chased losses from the nights before. Some came alive at the tables in ways they did not do elsewhere at other times.

Frank LeRoy was all of those people—and sometimes none of them—but tonight he was repaying a debt. He had slipped away from the careful ministering of Mangas by promising him he was on his way home and that he needed to appreciate the space to walk alone. The lights of *The Chrysalis* beckoned. Mangas gave way without too much argument on this occasion, although it was just possible that the sideway glances he had been receiving from the Waspero, Autumn Cork, as they watched the game from a makeshift touchline some ten metres apart, might have turned his attention somewhat. Autumn was wearing much the same kind of gear she had been wearing when they first encountered each other standing in the middle of the Niba, although, in truth, she was actually dressed more colourfully with a tighter range of clothes that clung to her impressive body. When Mangas realised she was waiting to be called on to the field of play he was intrigued, thinking that things would not end well for somebody. He thought that that somebody would not be Autumn Cork. He hoped, also, it would not be him.

She met him with dark eyes flashing.

"Stay with me," she said. "Watch me until the moon climbs higher. Then we can talk."

The debt that the mayor was repaying was money owed to Mangas, in fact, although the latter did not know it. Mangas had entrusted his savings from their mountain ventures to Frank to invest in the various shares of companies doing well in Nosinala. Such companies took more readily to the name of the mayor than they did to that of Mangas. Frank was having a run of bad luck that was lasting longer than usual; his own money was long gone—he was now dipping heavily into the funds he had received from Mangas. But, it wouldn't take long to make good the loss and Mangas need never know, he reasoned. Carson Wong saw the mayor arriving and he ushered him in personally.

"Good evening, Mr Mayor, may I escort you to your usual table? Why don't you start with a complimentary hundred from me? You are one of our most valued customers after all. I'll send you your usual drink. May good fortune attend you!"

Carson Wong wasn't just being solicitous for the sake of making more money. He genuinely respected Frank and he wanted him to win. There were plenty of other fools out there who would make his fortune; he didn't want to see the mayor struggling. Against all odds, and all that. But Carson Wong also felt uneasy about the mayor and some of his plans for the development of the town.

Frank sat down beside the roulette. He knew he was taking on the wheel and not the others sitting around the same table. He nodded to a few known acquaintances, sharing the same feelings, experiences, desires and misgivings. He didn't want to see too many punters; that way the wheel did not turn as often as it should. But he didn't want to see too few other gamblers either; there was a dynamic and pageantry that should be enacted. He saw Domino standing a little apart from the table. Frank slipped him chips to the value of fifty dollars and said, "We 'Mayors' must stick together. Good Luck!"

Domino's looseness of tongue and manner had evidently reached Frank's office but whilst Frank's clerks were outraged at the ridiculous aspirations of somebody they saw as nothing more than a tinker, Frank was amused and even supportive of the barrow-boy. Sometimes he wished he could just hand over the Badge of Office to the market-trader. It would be unburdening. Somebody would become the next mayor—why not Domino? But first, he had to win some money. Domino joined the game and sat opposite the mayor. Others joined in. The coloured wheel span one way and the white ball span the other. Thus did the game of chance begin.

Frank loved the decisive, yet soft, call of the endlessly polite croupiers just before they span the wheel: *Rien ne va plus.* The game of roulette had retained some aspects of its French origins in these parts. Often, Frank wished he had said 'No more bets' when he was on one of his losing streaks. But how does one know? *Rien ne va plus* would have been a good title for a novel, thought Frank, even if his better story would have been *Juste un pari de plus* or, to those operatic-loving souls still out there, *Encore! Encore! Encore*! He loved the clicking of the wheel and the clacking of the ball when they kicked against each other as their separate, yet entwined, momentums diminished. One could smoke at the roulette wheel. And one could drink. And one could gamble. The colours were black and red. The green of the table. And there was always the white of the ball. Just don't lean on the table. Get Lucky, or cheat, or develop a way to change the odds. Frank would never cheat. He would get lucky or change the odds.

A fellow punter leant towards Frank after he had suffered yet another severe loss.

"Do you know, they say that the numbers nought to thirty-six add up to '666'? And you must know who owns the number 666?"

Frank wanted to say 'Fuck off'—especially since they were playing American roulette where there were 38 pockets including the enticing 'double-O' but he spied the startling eminence of the croupier, who had now changed into a stylish woman, from the previous slick and sly male whom he had never liked, and so he smiled and put down double the amount of chips on the numbers he had just lost. He knew this was a loser's strategy but he wanted to say 'Fuck off' so he did it anyway. He lost again.

Carson Wong shimmered towards Frank's elbow.

"Why not stop now, Frank, and come back another time?"

Frank looked straight ahead at the table.

"This is absolutely *not* the time to stop! You know that, don't you? The ballistics are looking good. The numbers are due."

Frank asked the croupier for a thousand dollars of chips.

"In for a penny," he said, but he might have just about managed, "Pour un sou."

The clacking and the clicking of the wheel insistently hit the air once more. It was the sound of a familiar friend, an ancient foe. The colours green and red and black and white merged together like hallucinatory images and Frank heard and saw echoes of his hunters in the snow whose backs bent low and dejected even in the swirling magnificence of their vista. The sense of movement, yet also being caught in time, overwhelmed him, as it did the hunters.

Oddly, perhaps, the chips in front of Domino were stacking up in almost direct proportion to the downward spiral of the real mayor opposite him. Domino felt inclined to send fifty dollars' worth of chips towards the mayor but even his market-trader's ethics realised that this was not the right thing to do.

Go red. Or black. Or odds. Or evens. Or high or low. Or middle or left. Or right or outer or inner. Or cash in. Or just sit and watch for a while. Or go home. Or smile, graciously. Or gnash teeth, bitterly. Or wring hands ecstatically. The end result was always the same. But he went black. He saw the red squares but he wanted them painted black.

And Mayor Frank LeRoy encountered—what did he encounter?...in those early hours of the morning, when mistress and wife were wandering alone in their beds, without solace or comfort; when his dear friend Mangas was entering Waspero Autumn, the big man pre-destined; when his 'protégé' Domino was raking it in like a Casino-Veteran of the moment—the mayor, Frank LeRoy, encountered his moment of greatness which flickered and then faded, as the losses, the losses, advanced like waves.

The faltering steps of Frank LeRoy, the father, going home at daybreak with headache and heartache, did not encounter the bright steps of Bobby LeRoy, the son, skipping in the opposite direction at about the same time. Bobby had enjoyed the afternoon yesterday in the company of Eve, the new girl who had caught his attention, and her parents Mr and Mrs Horner, who were pleased that he was the son of the mayor—and therefore respectable—but not yet satisfied that he could be trusted alone with their daughter. So Peter and Polly Horner went wherever Bobby and Eve went. Eve was embarrassed and Bobby a little on edge but his decency and charm must have had some positive effect since Mr and Mrs Horner agreed that their daughter could meet up with Bobby, without them, the next day. They had not reckoned on the rendezvous time being daybreak but Eve jumped at the chance when Bobby suggested it before they departed the night before. The sun was already breaking through the low clouds when Bobby saw Eve waiting for him at the bend in the road. She waved and her bright eyes shone like precious stones.

"I can't believe we're out so early!" she exclaimed. "It's like we're the only two people up and about!"

"You wait till we get down by the river. There's a whole world there already moving and shaking off the dust."

Bobby was right. The market-traders were just putting the finishing touches to their stalls and small groups of people were wandering about though it wasn't entirely clear whether they were going home from the night before—like Frank—or arriving early for the day like Bobby and Eve.

Eve jumped up and down clapping her hands.

"Oh, I'm *so* excited!" she said. "Thank you for taking me out, Bobby!"

"Did you manage to get away alright? So early, I mean."

"Yes. The guests wanted early starts too. Mr and Mrs Saddles were making breakfast as I left! Everybody's talking about the festival! Mother and Father were also getting up. They were surprised I was dressed but they liked you, Bobby. 'Make sure he looks after you' they said as I was leaving. You will look after me. Won't you, Bobby?"

He took her hand. It seemed the most natural thing in the world.

Domino was nowhere to be seen in the marketplace; perhaps he was nursing a headache too from his celebrations of the night before. Some Border Control guards were talking to a group of Noz who had emerged from the river, it seemed. The lack of friendliness apparent in the tone of voices did not seem in keeping with the carnival spirit so Eve looked away. She could hear a train coming in.

"That's the first train of the morning," said Bobby, "Let's go and watch the people coming off."

They ran towards the station.

Mangas was walking some way off, hand-in-hand with the wild-looking woman known as Autumn. Her hair was bedraggled and she seemed to be sporting a cut on her forehead. Mangas laughed as he saw Bobby disappearing with a young girl and said out loud, "I only look after the mayor—the son can look out for himself!"

Autumn laughed too.

"So that's the mayor's son, is it? Quite right—let them alone. Besides, now I can look after you."

Autumn looked up at Mangas and he beamed.

"It's me who should be looking after you! Your head is bruising nicely. There'll be a big shiner there soon!"

"But did you think I played well? I nearly scored once. And I gave out a few bruises as well, didn't I?"

It was true. Autumn had played like a woman possessed. If Mangas had been moved by the woman standing in the water he was utterly besotted by the woman who plays like a warrior.

When she had finished her stint on the field of play, Mangas and Autumn had taken in some food and drink and walked about and talked. Mangas did not know he could talk so much. She drew it out of him. And he would not have known that it was foreplay. Eventually, they lay down in the long grass and they came to know each other, through the magic hours, by the river, until morning.

And so, the second day began. Storms were still threatening but the skies remained mostly clear and the ground remained dry.

Dolly had maintained her resolution to 'go silent' with Frank for a short time only. She had not answered his calls at first. Then she read his texts without replying. He had said he was sorry for not picking up her call. He had not seen it until later, he said. She knew that was a lie. She had seen him look at his phone on the porchway when she was ringing from her car on the roadside opposite. So why would he lie? Was he embarrassed? Was he feeling awkward? Should she not have phoned? There she was again—finding a way out for him. It was not for her to excuse him. He needed to do that by himself. Still, she had received a kind of apology. And he was trying to reach out to her. She would have to call him or see him. They would have no barriers between them. That had been her mantra to date.

Frank had gone back to his office after his disastrous night at *The Chrysalis*. He had a headache after his excessive drinking. Often the drinks increased in line with his losses and last night's roulette had incurred severe losses to go with his other recent bad luck. He didn't go home. His wife would have assumed he was at Cavendish Avenue. And he didn't go to Cavendish Avenue because he had not had contact with Dolly for a while and he felt a little conflicted. Things had been smoother with Mary and she seemed to be trying harder to make things work. He wanted to do things right by Mary even though she had tricked him so badly about Bobby. He had got over the pain even if the memory persisted but she was still Bobby's mother and she would have to provide for him so he had to provide for her. He should do right by both of them.

Frank barged into his office having had trouble unlocking the door. There was no one there at that early time of the morning. He half-expected to hear Mangas' voice saying, "Where have you been, Frank? I want to look after you." He wished he had heard Dolly say that. Or did he mean Mary? But there was no one there. They were just voices in his head. He walked through to the back room and looked up at his painting of the hunters returning. They, too, looked disappointed. Their heads and those of their dogs were bent low, for they were thwarted, heavy-footed, sidling past the fire-makers outside the inn, exchanging no greetings, the warmth of the fire not reaching them in the dirty snow. The hunters looked out over an elevated view of their home territory and they, themselves, were overlooked by Frank as he scanned the painting as he had done so many times before. It was almost as if he expected a different result. Perhaps some of the hunting men would now have large carcasses slung over their backs and they would be walking tall and proud. Perhaps their fellow countrymen and women fanning the flames of the fire would wave to them and invite them over for a drink. But they never did.

The eyes of the viewer could sense the movement from the inn and the fire to the hunters to the frozen valley below where villagers skated on the pond and other groups of people went about their business amongst the scattered dwellings and spreading landscape that led towards the jagged mountain peaks in the distance. Frank thought that he loved the painting so much because, despite the sense of frustration for the hunters, life went on and there would always be another chance. He looked again at the inn sign that was hanging awkwardly from one hook only. He wanted to mend it. The sign said: *This is the Golden Stag* and there was the dark figure of a hallowed saint, kneeling in supplication, as it always did, at the feet of the animal whose antlers held between them a shining cross. The halo over the sainted man's head shone too. The man was supposedly the patron saint of hunters—Eustace—who would endure hardships to come in his life. But Saint Eustace was committed to his calling. And so were the hunters. And so, for that matter, was Frank.

He was in too far now to get out. But he had to make a plan. He had to beat the system. And, like the hunters, he had to put food on the table for his wife and his son. He had to provide for them. The men trudging back into the painting and the man standing outside the picture looking in had no choice but to fulfil their obligations. And so the quest would continue.

The second day came and went without incident. The lacrosse match continued; the rains stayed away, though thunder rumbled occasionally in the skies further away and the towns of Nosinala revelled in the festival atmosphere. Frank LeRoy kept a low profile for most of the day pretending to work on administrative matters in his office—he put a sign up on the inner door of his office 'Do Not Disturb!' Mary LeRoy was busy all day entertaining different groups of lady friends. Bobby and Eve were having the time of their lives down by the river.

Domino came to just after lunch with the slight remnant of a headache having had the most wonderful dream about making massive profits on the roulette wheel the night before. Every colour he chose, every line, every section of the table on which he had put down his chips came up as a winner. The more he won, the bigger he made his stake which meant he kept on winning more and more. Other figures came and went in his shadowy dream but he just stayed at the table until the owner, Carson Wong, was called over by the excitement his winning was generating amongst other punters. They wanted some of the action. This must be a lucky table! And Domino must have brought the luck.

Carson Wong's casino was no different to the other gambling establishments—they reserved the right to close down tables if too much was going out, just as they asked some punters to leave if they were incurring too much debt. It was not in their interest to preside over excesses of either kind; they wanted a steady income without controversy. They knew they would win in the end. They could play the long game. Experience had taught Carson Wong that when passions ran high, other problems developed and then the authorities became involved, questions were asked and greater regulation came in. Much as he liked Frank LeRoy personally, he was also aware that the mayor's office was taking tighter control over the gambling industry. He wanted to keep the mayor 'on his side' but he was also one of those local businessmen who were wary of the changes that seemed to be forced upon them. Carson nodded to the croupier who declared, "Last bets for the night on this table, folks!" before watching the game play out and then overseeing the placement of a black cloth over the gaming wheel and table which signified the end of the play.

All these details were seen vividly in Domino's dream because he didn't just dream them out again in his slightly drunken stupor since they actually happened in reality. Domino came to realise that he really *had* won a great deal of money.

Carson called him into his private office.

"Domino, I am delighted for you! I can't remember when one individual has won as much money as you have done tonight! May I make a suggestion?"

Domino nodded in assent, quite stupefied and still buzzing high with adrenalin.

"I think it would be safer for you if you left your winnings with me. I shall write you a promissory note to show you that my intentions are honourable. It would not be wise for you to walk out of here with bags of cash. It is dark and there are boisterous spirits about. Besides, I actually don't have all that money available. You have broken the casino's bank! Why don't you go home quietly and sleep it off? I will instruct one of my security staff to accompany you. Come back tomorrow and we will arrange to have all the money transferred into an account of your choosing."

Domino went off in a bit of a dream and then had that same dream all over again in the comfort of his own bed.

And on the third day, he woke in the early afternoon to see the promissory note from Carson Wong folded on the table beside his bed.

Domino took a shower and dressed quickly; he had an appointment at *The Chrysalis.* His heart was thumping when he arrived at the doors of the casino. He parked his bike and went in. There was not much action at that time of day. He walked past the blackjack tables where a few elderly ladies were trying their luck. And he couldn't help glancing across to the roulette wheels. He smiled across at one of the croupiers there and she smiled back but he was fairly sure it wasn't one of the table managers he had played with the night before. He strode on towards Carson Wong's office. Another slightly oriental-looking man emerged to greet him.

"Can I help you, sir?" He asked.

"I'd like to see Mr Wong, please. He is expecting me."

Carson Wong came out of his office himself.

"Mr Domino! So good to see you! I had thought you might not yet be awake. Perhaps there is something on your mind, eh? Come this way, please, come this way, sir!"

Domino thought there was a new-found respect in Carson Wong's intonation of the word 'Sir'.

"Mr Wong, I had some strange dreams last night, I don't mind telling you!"

"Domino, call me Carson, please. Please, sit down, sit down! Did your dreams involve winning a little bit of money, my friend?"

Carson Wong was laughing.

Domino laughed too.

"So it wasn't a dream!" said Domino, running his hands through his hair. "I knew it wasn't a dream, really, especially when I saw this document by my bed!"

He waved the promissory note.

"*Mister* Domino, did you think you could not trust me? I am a man of my word. I have not been idle whilst you were sleeping. I have made all the necessary arrangements for this end. All funds are now available. If you can give me the details of the account you want the money to be paid, I shall expedite all connected matters. After all, we take your money quickly enough, do we not? We should surely pay up with as much speed."

"Thank you, Carson. My details are here."

He handed him an envelope.

"One thing troubles me, though, Carson. It concerns the mayor. I don't know if you knew but he slipped me a starting stake right at the very beginning when I started to play. He then stayed on for a while, too, but he lost all his money, I think. I remember him slipping away. How much was he down?"

"Ah, the mayor, the mayor. He doesn't make himself popular, does he?"

Carson knew the market-traders were being squeezed just as much as the casinos, as well as several other businesses in town.

"I can't really discuss another client's finances, I'm afraid. But let's just say that the mayor owes *The Chrysalis* a lot more than the relatively small amount he lost last night."

"I want to pay it off," said Domino, decisively.

"Pardon?" Carson said.

"I want to pay it off. I have enough money, don't I?"

"Oh, yes, even though he owes a great deal, *you* could pay it off ten times over. But is this something you really want to do?"

"Yes. It kinda feels right. Then I can move on. Besides, I might be mayor one day and—who knows?—I might be glad of a helping hand some time. Pay it off. Take the debt out of my money then transfer the rest."

So with that rather unusual agreement in place, the two men went about their business for the rest of the day.

The first thing Domino did was pay a visit to the swankiest clothes shop in the upper reaches of the town where he kitted himself out, on account, with a new set of everything he had had his eyes on for some time—but could not afford—including the best, most colourful waistcoat in the store.

As events transpired, Frank never got to hear about his slate being wiped clean. Would it have made a difference? Difficult to say. Some events seem to be pre-destined regardless of the ebbs and flows. That was certainly true of the flood when it came. And of other things that happened subsequently.

With the conviction of all men who have drunk too much—especially those whose fortunes are flowing inexorably into a downward spiral—Frank opened a fresh bottle of whisky to 'help the fiddle go better', as he put it, though quite what he meant he would have been at a loss to explain. Frank said 'cheers' to the hunters in the painting as he sipped the first glass and then sat down with his papers in front of him. He read his official contract that had been drawn up when he was first appointed mayor. Hah! He thought. Some clauses seem to have been kept by only one side of the signatories. Well, it's not too late to have the last say. He began to put into effect the plot he had hatched.

But first, he should contact Dolly. He just wanted to hear her voice.

Dolly was on the verge of phoning him and was both pleased and disappointed that that decision had been taken away from her when her phone rang. She could pretend to be busy but, since she was not, she answered.

"Frank," she said, "I've been meaning to phone."

"I'm sorry," he said.

Then there was silence.

"Well, we won't go into what for, just yet, but where have you been? How are you?" Dolly asked.

"I'm fine. And it's been tricky. Stuff to do and all that. But can we meet sometime? Can I come over to Cavendish Avenue?"

There was a pause.

"I think not," she said. "Things are tricky, as you say. Perhaps we both need some time."

Frank had not expected such an answer.

"What's happened? You sound different," said Frank.

"Perhaps I am different, Frank. That's why I need some time. You might as well know—somebody I knew a long time ago—before I met you—has been in touch. He wants me to go away with him."

It was Frank's turn to go quiet. He took another glass of whisky.

"That's fine, Dolly. You must do what you must do. Let's leave it at that. Don't try to contact me again."

And he terminated the call.

A tear ran down Dolly's cheek. Never mind the fact that *he* had contacted *her*, she knew that it was over.

He was a busy man. He was the mayor. He had things to sort out. Didn't Dolly realise that she was nothing to him if she couldn't provide comfort? He didn't need Dolly, after all. Sometimes a man has to carry his load and tread the path that is designated. He stood up in front of the painting and gulped down another whisky. Why didn't somebody fix that sign? Well, he would fix the things in his own life that were broken and then he might just fix the sign himself.

Frank picked up the shotgun normally carried by Mangas and he took the whisky bottle with him, also, before getting into his car. He checked the glove compartment and saw the picture of his wife and son. On a ledge below there was his handgun. He exhaled deeply and said, "What the heck!" before driving off along the highway that ran alongside one of the straight stretches of the Niba.

"We've got to get rid of him."

Perry Northrop was talking to Miles McKay. They had arranged to meet in *The Elgin.* They were in one of the private lounges reserved for special guests. Miles had wanted to take the matter to the full board but Northrop had insisted they meet alone.

"Let's just vote him out," said Miles.

"No, he's still got two years to run. He can do a lot of damage in that time. He has to go now."

"But how then?"

Northrop went quiet.

"There are ways and means."

"I still think the board should have a say. We've got that extraordinary meeting coming up to discuss the mayor's proposal for the development of the casinos. Why don't we bring it up then?"

"Look, Miles," said Northrop, beginning to lose patience, "You must hate the casino idea more than anybody! It's preposterous to allow any more Noz, let alone the natives, to have greater control in the casinos. I'd like to see them all run out of the place so that the likes of you and I—and other respectable Nosinalans—can manage them properly. Just because the mayor met with the chief to defuse the violence, it does not follow that we have to give away the casinos. They should be coming cap-in-hand to us!"

"But Frank gave his word."

"It was not his to give. Besides, a man's word does not count when one is dealing with aliens. The rules aren't the same. Every truce is followed by the breaking of a truce. We cannot always dictate the terms of a treaty but we can always determine the best time to break the terms."

"But what about honour?"

"They have sacrificed the right to honour. For that to apply, you have to be dealing with honourable men. It's a tough business, running a town, and if we left it to those south of the river, we'd soon be sailing down that river along with everything we've built up. This is a time for clear heads and steady hands, Miles."

Miles McKay certainly didn't want to lose his controlling influence with the leisure business and Northrop was right: he didn't want any other promises being made to the tribes or to the Noz.

"We can throw out the casino proposal at the meeting very quickly. We don't want to dilute the message with other business about the mayor. We can deal with this separately. Besides, if we handle the mayor properly, there will be no reason to have the meeting."

"What do you have in mind, Perry?"

"Well, let's just say that Nosinala can be a dangerous place if a man walks too late. Leave it with me."

But Perry Northrop didn't think for a second that it would be left to him alone. He thought that Carson Wong was on his side. And that Digger Brown was fed up with the mayor. As well as Hendrik van de Berg and the traders of the town in their shops and their stalls. And the Noz had every reason to hate him, as well as the tribes, despite this latest 'treaty'. And there was no love lost with the officials and agents of Border Control. Why, even his own marshals didn't like him! Northrop was firmly of the opinion that the mayor's time had come and gone. He had certain men who would do his bidding.

The third day of the festival ran on in splendid heart. And so did the fourth day. The lacrosse match stood at eight goals apiece, although there had been some disputes until the Elders were called upon to make their judgement. But the rains had started to fall. The storms that had already wreaked havoc further upstate now seemed bent on turning their attention on Nosinala. Slight showers had fallen through the afternoon of the fourth day but as the evening descended the rain increased with the darkness and by true night the storm took hold. The match was suspended for the night. People turned in or flocked to the bars and casinos. The market stalls had been packed away. The forecast was gloomy for the next few days. The anticipated deluge had begun.

Upstate, river tributaries had already merged into one, increasing the flow and power of their normal courses. There were tales of localised flooding. Two men had lost their lives trying to rescue stranded cattle on a river bend. And into this scenario, the Second-Chancers kept pouring back, too. There had been a steady trickle of them ever since Frank's ordinance, implemented by Colonel Wesley Harding's agents, had been enforced. Hank Starling patrolled the border zones constantly but there had been increased activity recently. The Buffer Boys were becoming more and more agitated. And the tribesmen and women—those warriors who were not always accountable to the restraining influences of their chiefs—were also increasingly hostile and reckless. The rains continued to pour down throughout the fourth night and long into the morning of the fifth day.

The Lacrosse Festival seemed set for an early finish. The extraordinary meeting of the board took place as planned, but not with the mayor's single agenda point about the casinos and the promise to allow the tribesmen greater control, but with a hastily convened proposal that the Lacrosse Festival should be brought to an end. Despite the potential loss of income, all board members agreed that there was little option. The waters of the Niba were rising to dangerous levels. The playing area where the match had been played was already flooded with patches of swampy water. There was no point now in setting up the market stalls again. Those who were camping had already left. The strain was being put on the upper town to contain and provide for the influx of people seeking shelter and things to do. Severe weather warnings were being issued by authorities further away and the centre of the storm seemed to be hurtling towards them. Events were moving quickly.

The mayor had not been seen for a while. The board thought it a poor show that he did not turn up for the meeting he had arranged even if the agenda point had changed. Perry Northrop had a quiet word with Miles McKay on their way out.

"*Now* do you see the wisdom of my proposal? The mayor is on his way out. Watch this space."

Mary LeRoy had been approached by Winnie Crane and by Reverend Hopkins as to Frank's whereabouts. She was embarrassed on several fronts to confess that she did not know for sure where he was. She made something up along the lines of, 'I think he mentioned something about going hunting and fishing,' but neither Winnie nor William was persuaded by the story. Mary drove straight to Cavendish Avenue when they had gone.

When she arrived in the suburbs, she saw a man putting suitcases into the back of a car. She walked right past him and stormed into Dolly's house.

"Where is he?" She screamed.

Dolly was taken aback.

"Mary! What are you doing here?"

"Don't give me that! Where is my husband? Where is Frank!"

"I haven't seen Frank for days, maybe weeks. The last message I had from him told me not to contact him again. And the last time I saw you two together you were kissing and cuddling on a couch! He's not with me, Mary. Perhaps he never was."

Mary looked around her in Dolly's house in which she had never taken a single step before but she could see that Dolly was leaving. There were boxes and cases standing by the doorway. The house looked stripped of home comforts. It was empty and bare. As a woman, she wondered what she had been lacking, other than her original deceit about Bobby, what was it that was so abhorrent that it had driven her husband into this soulless, barren place, into the arms of this woman?

"Where are you going?" She asked Dolly.

Dolly felt like saying 'I'm Dolores Bellworthy, once of Cavendish Avenue, just a sad-eyed lady of the lowlands, and it's none of your goddamn business where I'm going!' What she actually said was, "I'm leaving town. For good. I'm going east. Goodbye, Mary. In another life, we could have been friends, you know. We both loved the same man, after all."

The man who had been packing the trunk of the car stepped into the entrance. This was a man who was clearly not Frank LeRoy.

"Well, darling, are you ready? Shall we just push on? We've got a long way to go and the storm is getting worse."

Mary turned and left without ceremony. The storm was getting worse.

And the storm really was getting worse.

The Niba was already unrecognisable. Three nights ago, Autumn Cork had whispered softly to her new love Mangas, "How strangely still the water is today. It is not good for water to be so still that way." She could have been drawing on some ancient tribal wisdom or she could have been quoting from a modern-age poet who recognised the plight of the downtrodden. Now, the waters of the Wanageeniba were boiling and hissing, spitting like a writhing snake whose time had come after ages of crawling on its slippery belly down below the edges of the land. Rivers were meant to ebb and flow. They needed currents and splashing and the sounds of life unfettered. They needed to flood every now and then.

Mangas had also been looking for Frank. It was his job. He was paid to do that. But it had nothing to do with the money. He didn't care for money. He would have entrusted all his money to Frank. In fact, he *had* given over the bulk of his money to Frank. Didn't they own shares together in some venture which would bring dividends when they were old? But Mangas was worried. Not about the future, but about the present. Frank went off sometimes hunting and fishing, it was true. But normally, they went together. Or Frank went with his beloved son. *Their* hunting and fishing were much more productive than the deflated hunters in Frank's painting. When Mangas and Frank LeRoy hunted, they always came back as better men. They might have caught something or there might just have been tales of what-could-have-been. But they bonded as friends and they experienced life all around them as it was meant to be lived.

It wasn't even a man-thing. Mangas would happily have gone hunting with a woman. He was engaged now in a 'hunt', a dance, if you like, with a woman who exceeded all his dreams. The night before, Mangas and Autumn had looked out over the blackness of the river and somehow he sensed that she wanted to swim. Mangas had dreaded this moment, even in the short time they had known each other.

"Well, shall we?" She said.

Mangas tried to sound like a river god a little tired of the wet but he suspected that his words seemed like the croaking of the last frog.

"We could just look and marvel at the depths before us."

"Oh, but the depths below are so much better! Come on! I want you to rescue me! Let's plunge together!"

Autumn waded and then dived into the Niba.

"Oh, God!" thought Mangas, though he wasn't sure if he had said it aloud.

He entered, she splashed, he struggled, she clung onto him.

A look of recognition passed over her face.

"Oh, darling," she said, "You can't swim, can you?"

She clung to him and he held onto her and they rolled together.

"One day—or one night—I will teach you to swim," she said.

"None of the gods can swim," he said.

"Oh, but they can! That's where they come alive!"

Once, Frank, Bobby and Mangas had all hunted together but it seemed to lose something of its allure. It might have been a generational thing. But that could not have been true since Frank and Bobby had had so many rewarding times together in the foothills and the forests and the streams of the county and beyond. And it had nothing to do with family because Mangas and Bobby had also enjoyed some energising times on the trail. Although only Frank and Mary—and Mangas, as it happens—knew that Bobby and Frank were not strictly 'family' in the biological sense of the word. The hunting in threes was perhaps the problem. If one was to expose one's soul to another, using shotguns and slingshots and traps, in the rivers and the mountains and the prairies of life, holding hands, metaphorically, and talking into the night, under twinkling stars and the thudding canvas, gently flapping in the night-air, whilst owls and ground night-hunters hooted and swooped, with the 'left-far-behind' noise of fabricated sound thumping dully in the memory only, perhaps the experience should be shared by two and no more.

Whatever the philosophy, Mangas knew well enough that the hunter could make many mistakes but the hunted only one. Something told him in his bones that Frank had become the hunted.

Which was why he was hunting for Frank LeRoy, his friend and his mayor.

Mangas went to the office and was puzzled because his shotgun was gone. There were few signs of agitation other than the fact that the painting of The Hunters was hanging slightly off-kilter. Mangas corrected the alignment of the painting and looked about him. The shotgun was gone; the door was ajar. The car keys were missing from their usual hook. A hand-written note from Frank would have been useful but, since none existed, Mangas got in his car and drove to Cavendish Avenue. When he arrived, he saw the seemingly mad figure of Mary LeRoy speeding past him like a woman possessed. And when he drew up alongside 24A Cavendish Avenue, he saw Dolly and a man not named Frank draw away from the road. Dolly was texting a message to Frank saying, 'Why didn't you come?' Dolly and the man drove off.

Frank would not be here. Frank could only be on the road. He would be hunting and fishing. He would be down at the river bend. But they never went there together. It was Frank's special place. It was where Frank never caught any fish.

Because it was here that Frank was not looking to catch. It was here that Frank was waiting to be caught. Mangas drove quickly to the Niba Bend. It was five miles out of town. Nobody went there. It was deeper and darker and more dangerous than anywhere else on the river. If Frank wasn't at home with his wife, who probably loved him, or at Cavendish Avenue with his mistress, who possibly loved him, he would be at the bend of the Niba, which certainly loved him in an obsessive kind of way, just as Frank loved the Niba.

When Mangas arrived at the river bend—the Niba-Bend or the *Fork-that-Flatters* as the tribes would have it—he could see a car parked on a slight rise overlooking the river a little way off below. He drew closer and could see it was Frank's car. The engine was running and all windows were closed. Frank was slumped over the steering wheel and the doors were locked. There was an empty bottle of whisky on Frank's lap. Mangas knocked loudly on the window. There was no response. Mangas was nothing if not decisive. And powerful. He went quickly to the rear window and smashed it open with a rock. Mangas could do things like this. He got into the car, switched off the engine and slapped Frank about the face whilst shouting, "Frank! Frank! Wake up!"

But Frank did not wake up.

Mangas dragged him out of the car towards the river, and after taking a few steps into the water, he plunged the head of the comatose mayor into the Niba. Mangas then hauled Frank out by the hair and threw him onto the bank. He slapped him again. No response. He pressed Frank's chest and gave him the kiss of life. Later, he was to reflect on the sweet fact that the last lips he had kissed before Frank's were those of the divine Autumn Cork when they rolled together in the reed beds but that was not the observation that came to his mind in the moment. Frank *had* to live. That was Mangas' job—keeping him alive. They hadn't come this far just to die this way. Mangas wasn't sure what way would be better but it was not this, not now, by the banks of the Niba at the *Fork-that-Flatters.* Perhaps death by mountain bear would be better. Or worse. For that was how Frank had saved *his* life up in the mountains a long time ago. This was not the death destined for Frank. *That* bear had got Mangas cornered and he smelt blood.

Mangas had fallen on a rock and gashed his leg. The blood was flowing freely and Mangas' rifle was far away. The bear saw an easy prey. Frank came running out of the foliage where they had made camp. He had not had time to grab his shotgun either. All he had seen was Mangas and the bear, the bear and Mangas. Frank decided in an instant to turn the bear into the hunted. Frank became the hunter. He made himself big. He made loud noises. He advanced towards the bear. The bear was so startled by this apparently mad creature crashing out of the undergrowth, screaming unnatural sounds like an unknown demon from the forest, that he swung rapidly away into the thicket beyond Mangas and beyond this strange advancing threat which he did not recognise. The bear disappeared with a crashing of leaves of his own and Frank roared over the prostrate form of his friend who simply lay there bleeding and bemused.

What had just happened? Had Frank really just frightened off a bear that was about to kill him? That was about the measure of things. Frank patched up Mangas' wound as best he could with leaves and mulch from the forest floor and dragged him back to the rescue centre, on a crude, makeshift sleigh he had fashioned out of fallen timber and twine, at which place of refuge the proper medical attention could be administered. Mangas walked with a slight limp thereafter for the rest of his life but the important thing was that he was alive. The strangest thing of all was that the two men never spoke of the incident again.

All that happened a long time ago.

But it was Mangas, now, who was bringing his friend back to life, too. Mangas slapped Frank some more and he prayed to the spirits and he kissed him again and he blew life into his lungs. And whatever magic was circling in the air at that time, it worked, and Frank finally awoke out of his drunken coma and spluttered onto the ground and the whisky and the water fell out of his mouth. Frank gasped for air, he grasped the chance for life. He lived and survived. This was not the way to die after all. Mangas fell into a heap and screamed at the sky and his anguished howl might even have been heard as an echo in the mountains far away.

Mangas then shouted at Frank, "Why are you killing yourself this way, you bastard, you fool!"

Frank was rubbing his face and gulping down some water from the Niba.

"What are you talking about? I'm not killing myself. That's the last thing on my mind."

Mangas wanted to punch him.

"What about the engine? The locked doors? You were completely out! I had to drag you out of the car!"

Frank looked blank as if he was trying to remember a dream.

"Mangas, Mangas, my friend," he said in a soothing voice, "I drank too much, that's all. I must have fallen asleep.

I remember waking up cold. I turned on the engine. I must have fallen asleep again. It was a rough night."

"Why did you lock the doors?"

"No idea. Perhaps I thought I was going to be eaten by a bear. Who knows? I was drunk. Drunks do silly things. Perhaps I thought I was going to be attacked by wild men. Men are worse than bears, you know. There are plenty of people out there who might like to kill me—I don't need to do it myself."

He laughed sardonically.

"Don't talk like that," Mangas said. "Let's go back."

Mangas decided to leave his own car there and drive Frank back to the office in Frank's vehicle. Frank would have a chance to make himself presentable—he looked like a hobo—and Mangas could tidy up the inside of Frank's car which did not look like it belonged to a mayor. Mangas took the route along the dust track that skirted the course of the river. He could see from a distance a large crowd of people gathered by the banks of the Niba. It was a strangely biblical scene. The onslaught of rain and the storms upstate had caused the tributaries of the Niba to flood in, like horizontal waterfalls, towards the mother river, and humanity and water had seemed to confluent in swollen, raging, ugly narratives demanding something like resolution or retribution, perhaps.

But there were no waterfalls here, just lots of white water and brown water and blue-black water cascading and conjoining into a separate and single identity of its own so that the whole mass became a new organism with a capricious will that seemed malevolent, though its reality was that it remained supremely indifferent. It was greater than the blood-flow of the ancient gods—it simply didn't care. But Mangas cared.

And Frank cared. Mangas might have driven on if the mad circumstances of their predicament had been dealt more conventional cards. But, in the dark auspices of the moment, when the skies aligned in portents of doom, he seemed compelled to stop. There had been a momentary let-up in the falling rain, too. And the wind had dropped. This was one of those famous pauses that the clouds and the river and the *Skanze* created when a pause was needed.

Frank was singing—or growling—softly in a low deep voice that would occasionally rise to the level of an operatic baritone. When he sang louder, he turned his head and smiled triumphantly or gratefully in the direction of Mangas. Frank was still partially, or wholly, drunk. The spectrum of drunkenness is an interesting one deserving of further analysis another time. Mangas wanted to slap Frank one more time but he stopped the car nevertheless, not, in fact, to smack his friend, but to investigate the oddness of the scene before them.

There appeared to be about a dozen or more Border Control agents looking agitatedly across the river. Some others were guarding the bridge that spanned that part of the Niba. The river was running as high as Mangas could remember and the inky-black waters were rushing by and swirling up the soft red mud from the banks and creating a confusion of colours and movement as white spouts broke over the broken stones further out mid-river. Mangas and Frank got out of their car. They could now see a couple of figures in the water struggling to swim. There was another throng of some twenty or thirty people—maybe more—scattered along the bridge towards the southern side. They were perhaps one hundred metres away.

Try to remember that there was no exactitude of forensics at work here. There was a weirdly dark daytime sky full of rumbling clouds racing unnaturally quickly. There was a raging river not seen before in living memory. There were enraged people with passions and prejudices just bursting with explosion. And Frank was there, too, with a capacity and a derangement dancing to the tune of the river gods.

The group from the south was made up of disgruntled Noz, vain-glorified tribesmen and the brooding desperation of the Second-Chancers. There were Buffer Boys and Jackals. And there were Esperillos and Conchillas. And representatives of tribes like the Wasperos. And, of course, the raw anger of the Border Control agents. And slowly, the otters and the eels slunk into the river. The noise level increased. The people were randomly yelling, the agents were shouting their curses angrily back and the river was booming and bursting. Cars belonging to the Border Control agents were flashing their bright orange warning lights fixed to their roof-fronts. More and more men were arriving in cars with sirens blaring, amongst them Marshal Canton and his sidekick Pointmoor.

Hank Starling saw Frank and Mangas approaching.

"Mr Mayor! Didn't expect you of all people! Things are getting a bit ugly here."

It transpired that a growing band of southerners was trying to take advantage of the distractions of the Lacrosse Festival and now the lull in the storm by crossing the river without going through the usual checkpoints. They had no identifying papers. Some were carrying bundles which they had refused to surrender for inspection. Some were bearing weapons which they brandished in threatening ways. The first agents manning the watchtower and the barrier gates had been forced back across the bridge by the surging crowd that was becoming more agitated. Radio calls had gone out for assistance and Starling and his agents had responded.

One newly arrived agent had pushed a young Noz into the river. A Second Chancer had jumped in to save the boy but both were now struggling in the fast-flowing current. A group of tribesmen had arrived and were shouting loudly. Autumn Cork could also be seen amongst the tribal warriors—most of whom were merely youngsters themselves—and she was trying to calm them down. She was moving quickly in the throng urging them to put down their weapons. Another Noz jumped into the river and the crowd came forward menacingly on the bridge.

The rain had started up again and was falling in horizontal sheets obscuring vision and distorting shapes and distance. The figures of people were smudged in intermittent mist, then seen again as a patch of clearness broke through, only to become half-hidden once more as the shadowy film of sweeping rain intensified. A gunshot rang out from the southern side of the bridge. There was more hollering and whooping. Stones were being thrown by the crowd and were now falling around the feet of the agents who were poised with their guns at the ready. One stone glanced against the lower leg of an agent.

Hank Starling instructed his men to fire a warning volley over the heads of the angry crowd. A stray ricochet from an agent's bullet seemed to have struck the shoulder of one of the tribesmen, too. He had fallen to the ground and a figure could be seen bending over him. Frank saw the figure reach for what looked like a rifle. On his side of the bridge, nobody seemed to be doing anything. He could make out the faces of Canton and Pointmoor, looking green and red, as they clearly saw, as he did, the figure opposite them raise what looked like a rifle in his direction. They did nothing. They might even have been smiling, slyly.

At such moments, it is remarkable how time seems to stand still and all kinds of observations can race across one's mind. Even as Frank was raising his own gun to shoot, he was thinking about the expressions on the faces of Cant and Pointless and wondering whether reptiles like them took on the same countenances as each other through close proximity in their working lives or through merely being simpletons. Mangas, at least, was moving quickly towards Frank, determined to protect him from the bullet that was evidently coming. Frank levelled his own shotgun which he had previously fetched from his car and fired the gun in the direction of the figure before he was fired upon himself.

Somebody shouted, "Let's break the chains!"

There were colours spinning, colours of red and black, and the green background of the river clashed and then melted into the whiteness of the cloud edges trying to break through.

The figure fired upon slumped to the ground. It was Autumn Cork. She died instantly and her body then slipped from the bridge into the river.

The death of Autumn Cork could have provoked a massive insurgence in retaliation or it could have stunned everybody into suspended animation. It was the latter reaction that prevailed. As the slow-motion moments unfolded disproportionately to the actual chronological time elapsing, Hank Starling could be heard shouting at the mayor, "Get out of here! Get away! You shouldn't be seen anywhere near this scene! Go!" He had the presence of mind to be horrified at the implications of the mayor, himself, shooting one of the aliens.

Frank blinked and then ran to his car. The keys were still in the ignition. He felt drunk no longer, revved the engine, slipped into gear clumsily and then raced off leaving clouds of dust in his wake to add to the general obfuscation. The Noz and the tribesmen had decided to run for their lives back to their southern outposts from which they had come. Mangas had had no time to join Frank so he ran over to the fallen figure on the bridge around whom others had now gathered, including Sheriff Nail who might have been there all along or might have only just arrived to pick up the pieces yet again. The figure who had taken a hit to the shoulder from the ricochet of a stray agent's bullet earlier sat bleeding but upright on the edge of the bridge.

"She was trying to take my stick," he said. "She was trying to help me stand up. She wanted us to stop. She was dead before she fell into the river. She died for me."

It was Rondo who was talking, the son of the Conchilla chief, Red, who was still relying on a walking stick as he continued to recover from the beating he had received some days before.

In the silence that followed, it became clear that the would-be-assassin who had lifted a rifle to shoot the mayor was in fact the peace-keeping Autumn Cork who was holding a stick. Mangas heard all this and knew that his new-found love was now swimming with the spirits of the Niba. It would be a futile gesture to dive into the river to bring her back even if he could have found her body, even if he could swim. She could have been the one who had saved him but he could not save her in the end. But Mangas knew that Frank had killed her. And Frank had just driven away from the scene of the crime. Mangas ran back to his own car and sped towards Frank's office; that was where he would go, for sure.

The rain returned with a vengeance and the wind had also picked up. Exactly *what* the wind had picked up wasn't entirely clear. It is a strange phenomenon that the vagaries of the weather and the manifestation of human behaviour appear to be inextricably linked. This duality of nature—environmental and human—begs the question as to which storm presages which. Did the events of that day, perhaps all days, unfold because of the weather or did the gods send in the tempest to match the deeds of men? No matter, really. The players were now set on a course that would converge much as when the fated *RMS Titanic* met the indifferent iceberg.

Frank drove directly to his office because it was the nearest and safest place to get away from the violence that might have ensued had he stayed at the bridge. He had shot someone. And he was the mayor. He was an easy target of hatred for those who were discontented at the best of times—and these were not the best of times. He was not to know that the killing of Autumn Cork—nor even, of course, that it was Autumn Cork he had killed—acted not as a catalyst but as a sobering coagulant that slowed the blood flowing in the veins of those who would otherwise be exacting revenge.

Besides, the rain was continuing to stream down from the inky-black skies and news was coming in, independently, to those at the bridge, that a protective levee further upriver had collapsed, thus creating fresh cascades of wild torrents that were heading their way. Frank slammed the door shut behind him and ran into his inner office. He had to think quickly. Was this the moment—that he had planned—to end things? He picked up his copy of Yeats and *An Irish Airman Foresees His Death* fell open …*I balanced all, brought all to mind, the years to come seemed waste of breath, a waste of breath the years behind in balance with this life, this death.*

The Second Coming was the next poem that caught his attention as he flicked through the pages…

Turning and turning in the widening gyre
The falcon cannot hear the falconer
Things fall apart; the centre cannot hold;
Mere anarchy is loosed upon the world,
The blood-dimmed tide is loosed, and everywhere
The ceremony of innocence is drowned;
The best lack all conviction, while the worst
Are full of passionate intensity.

Too much Yeats, clearly, wasn't good for one's frame of mind. *Think clearly, man!* he shouted to himself. He needed a gun—whatever might happen next. He found it reassuring and empowering to grip more tightly on his revolver. He pressed the nuzzle next to his head. But he could not, would not, simply kill himself. That was not the plan. "My love will laugh with me before the morning comes," he said to himself. He needed someone else. A stranger. Or someone he could trust absolutely. He lowered the gun and looked across the room at the painting on the wall. The hunters looked more dejected than ever. Was he going mad? Did he suffer from some mental derangement that led him towards thoughts of suicide? He was not responsible for his actions. He was insane. *Non compos mentis* as the legal definitions might have it. But he felt more responsible and clear-headed than ever.

The buffalo come in throngs and they will cover you—so went the ancient saying amongst hunters everywhere—but there were no buffalo or any other kind of prey being dragged behind them, in the painting, by the downtrodden hunters, trudging still through the heavy snow. Frank looked more closely at the principal hunter who was dangling, disconsolately, what might have been a brace of pheasants, or possibly a hare, from the staff held over his right shoulder. He wanted to look beyond the hunters' slow steps—as did the hunters—but Frank couldn't help noticing something he had not seen before in all the years he had studied the painting. The hunter's staff was pointing directly at the broken sign above the inn door. How could he have missed that?

Frank had seen the broken sign so many times before but he had never picked up on the sad and understated empathy of the hunter's staff. The hunter in the painting knew that the inn sign was broken but he could not fix it. Or, more accurately, the walking pole on the hunter's shoulder knew that the inn-board was broken. It was making a sign of its own. The hunter was walking on by, incapable of action, just as he could no longer organise a successful hunt. Frank and the hunter were one and the same. Their reason for living had been taken away. But unlike the hunter, Frank could still fix things in the remaining minutes of his life even if he could not ever fix the broken sign.

He was not insane. He just needed a sign of his own.

And Mangas did not let him down. It would be Mangas, wouldn't it? At that moment, Mangas burst through the door to the office, mad with rage, carrying his own shotgun and shouting, "Frank! Frank!"

Frank smiled.

"At last! We can set things right, you and I!"

Mangas smouldered.

Frank handed him his gun.

"You have to kill me. Shoot me, then disappear. They won't come looking for you. They know there are plenty of other candidates out there. And I will die in the service of the state. That is important. Then my wife and son will get my pension. I can do right by them. I've thought this all through, Mangas, you don't need to look alarmed!"

Mangas couldn't believe what he was hearing.

"Frank, I *have* come here to kill you!"

"That's what I'm saying! Good! Do it!"

"No, Frank, what I'm saying is that I chased after you to kill you because you killed the woman I loved!"

"What are you talking about? Do you mean Autumn? I know you have feelings for Autumn but she will still be here for you. She can love you too. Do this for me and you can be together."

"We cannot be together. You killed her by the bridge."

Frank suddenly realised what Mangas was saying.

"Wha…at?! No! It couldn't have been her! Say it wasn't her!"

From the look on Mangas' face, Frank knew that it was her.

There followed a few moments of silence when each man looked the other up and down and each man wondered what to do next.

Frank walked towards Mangas and embraced him. Frank was crying.

"I am so sorry, *so* sorry! I didn't know! How could I know, my friend? The rain was blinding! All I could see was a figure about to shoot! Mangas! You've got to believe me!"

Mangas did believe him, though he didn't want to cut any slack to the man who had killed his new-found love. Mangas believed him because the rain *was* blinding and he didn't know, himself, that it was Autumn on the other side of the bridge and he couldn't tell, either, that the 'weapon' she was pointing in their direction was just a walking stick belonging to Rondo. But it is difficult for a man to remain rational when tragedy strikes.

Frank pointed to the gun that was now in Mangas' hand.

"It is even more important, now, that you should kill me! Mangas, I am asking you as your dearest friend to do this for me. For us both. For Autumn. For my wife and son. A tooth for a tooth, and all that. Please squeeze the trigger."

Mangas quickly raised the barrel of the pistol towards Frank's head. His hand shook for a moment and then he slowly lowered his arm.

"I can't," said Mangas. "You saved my life. It cannot end like this between us."

"Well, I shall do it, then. But you must remove the gun from my hand afterwards. It must look like murder. You must wipe it clean and you must wipe off your own prints too. Take it where it can be found. Even a verdict of 'murder by persons unknown' will suffice."

The two men looked at each other, eyes squinting and moist.

A curtain at the window flapped in the wind and they both could hear the rain pounding on the roof and walls.

A gunshot rang out and filled the room. Frank fell to the floor, dead. Mangas rushed forward to help him and the gun fell to the floor, too. But were there other guns pointing through the chinks in the curtains and were there really footsteps running away outside? Or was that just a sensation from the shadows and the thunder and the rain and the wind combining in some operatic howl of justice meted out by the gods? What did Frank say he had to do? The gun! He had to get rid of the gun. He left the inner office in panic but slowly gathered his thoughts as he ran, limping, ever closer to the river, now flash flooding with the storms and the fresh deluge of water and mud from the collapsed levees. There could be no other ending.

The rain lashed down and the winds seemed to have increased. He let the gun slip from his grasp as he reached the lapping edges of the Niba. And he pulled from his neck the emblem of the snake that he had worn, faithfully, ever since the girl, with the big, grateful eyes—whom he had saved from the river—gave it to him by the market stalls what seemed like a lifetime ago. He let that fall, too, on the banks of the Niba, where it mingled with the sand and the scree and the bare, wet rocks that were devoid of life.

"The river," he said, unnecessarily.

Improbably, there was a hillbilly busker sheltering under the low branches of a river tree sending plangent violin strains out over the river plains and Mangas, oddly, stooped to drop some coins into his hat lying crumpled on the floor.

"Thanks—appreciate it!" was all the busker said.

He was otherwise caught in a world and time of his own. And this long-haired youth was so beautiful. Perhaps he was a river god representing the 'what-might-have-been'. Or was he simply accompanying the past or ushering in the future? Frank had told Mangas that in the old Homeric writings rivers were personified. They became characters in the story. Was this boy part of the river? Was he a watery element sucked ashore for a while to sit in the dust and play sweet tunes on his violin so that passers-by could drop spare coins—or ignore him as they chose? It could be more than that. He could be collecting votive offerings before slipping back into the river whence he had come—the origin and final destination of all life. It could have been less than that—he could have just been a washed-up busker, a bum, with nothing better to do.

Mangas walked on because the random choices we make don't only belong to the broken gods in Greek myths. The long strands of the busker's hair, thicker than the strings of his violin, rippled in the wind, playing different silent tunes of their own. Mangas filled his pockets with the largest stones he could find and started walking into the river. The water was cold but what was that to this big, strong man, this hunter, this man of inner passion who had lost his love?

As the swirling levels rose against his thighs, his chest, he raised his arms high like times before though, this time, he was carrying nothing except the knowledge of what had passed and the stones that became heavy in his pockets. He kept on walking and the current, flowing more strongly now, made his steps unsteady. He couldn't be sure whether or not there was somebody standing on the other side of the river. The margins of the river edges had widened; it was too far to see across. He waved anyway. He stumbled, fell face-first into the water and swallowed. He rose quickly into the air and gasped. It was not so bad, this river. He lost his footing again as the harsh winds of the Skanze whipped up the waters of the

Niba and the Wanageeniban gods were suddenly swimming all around him, all-consuming like the great silence and the great anguish within him, as he felt the pull on his bones. Two minutes later, Mangas was gone, with bubbles, only, frothing and bursting on the surface of the river.

Autumn and Mangas had been different but their lives were interconnected. Perhaps one can imagine Mangas happy like a Sisyphean figure relieved of his burden; perhaps he was just swirling in a subconscious state towards the bottom of the river but he had found, briefly, a sense of love—and himself—in the difference.

Just about the time that Mangas was limping into the Niba with his stone-laden pockets and his mind swirling with images of his deceased best friend, Frank, and his beloved Autumn Cork, also dead, the tribesfolk south of the river were engaged in a ceremonial dance of their own. The dance was wild and sapient, fired by hallucinatory drugs that led to trances that revealed the cosmos. Their faces were stained with ochre which seemed to make their gods specific and universal in the glare of the burning fires. Young men were trying to outdo each other with shows of strength and athletic manoeuvres. Horses were being raced on impromptu dust-tracks. Women in colourful clothes were chanting and dancing in unison, the rags of their skirts streaming around them like snakes. And the old men were watching, contentedly. Something was moving in the skies and on the plains. Their gods were inside them.

Sheriff Nail had just captured a jackal whose trail he had been following for a while. The rain dripped off his hat and poncho onto the pathetic figure of the jackal who lay bleeding at the feet of the sheriff who was holding a gun over his head.

"Is there any way out of this, Sheriff?" He pleaded, in the whine of a cornered animal.

"Sorry, son, I'm an Old Testament kind of guy—an eye for an eye, you piece of filth!"

Sheriff Nail aimed his gun at the jackal's face and pulled the trigger as he intoned the words, "Lord Jesus Christ, Son of God, have mercy on me, a sinner." It wasn't clear whether the prayer was for himself or the jackal.

With his gun still smoking, the sheriff went back to his hut and then decided to join the tribes in their dance ceremonies. He started participating in his own way from a short distance. The rain now stopped. He had brought his chair and he could sing the tunes even if he didn't know the words. He drank red wine from a vessel that resembled nothing so much as a chalice. He could have been the high priest adding credibility to the proceedings.

In the shadows, it would not have been surprising to see the anguished figure of Reverend William Hopkins, breaking bread, and also contributing with his particular brand of incantations. The spirit of the reverend raised a glass to the sheriff—and was that Molly Doyle, too, shimmering under the haze of the broken light? Autumn Cork would surely have been there had she not been shot. And Mangas would have been there, too, had he not been drowned.

In the aftermath, the Nosinalans had been stunned into a great silence which was odd given the nature and preponderance of violence latent in that place. It was as if something more important had died that day. The bodies of Autumn Cork and Mangas had been found two days later, in the river, strangely entwined, caught on the branches of two osculating, free-floating logs that might not have saved them from drowning but had, at least, trapped their separate experiences of death in a symbiotic moment of time. Domino dragged them from the river and felt the overwhelming need to do something useful with the rest of his life. The body of Frank LeRoy, the mayor, had been discovered in his office by Marshal Canton and his deputy, Pointmoor.

There were footprints and there was evidence of gunshots from within the room and from the direction of the window. A well-thumbed book of the poetry of Yeats lay open on the floor. A painting had fallen from the wall and there was scattered glass everywhere. The hunters were still crestfallen and the snow still lay white and grubby on the ground. And as for the broken inn sign? Well, it still hung broken in the painting, of course, but the way it was lying on the floorboards of the office, 45 degrees to the left, had rendered it seemingly upright at last and it was the rest of the painting, therefore, that was out of kilter with the inn sign. The hunters looked elevated and the heads of the hounds that were black were no longer drooping.

The winter trees bent leftwards, it was true, and the skaters on the ice were clinging on precariously to a new configuration but the whoosh of the wind had created a new cross-section of reality which might just have combined with the green-grey skies and the red streaks of the bricks, the fire, a few lean dogs, to suggest that the actuality had tilted happily to the left of centre too. The sign of the inn had at last returned to the horizontal.

Not that Cant and Pointless noticed any of that.

The busker was still sitting by the riverside playing some resonating tunes of jazz and blues on his violin before standing up and then walking off into a cluster of feathery trees whose branches drooped into the water. The trees could have been two thousand years old, symbols of souls aspiring to heaven whilst weeping into the waters and the land on earth. Then, again, they could just have been trees.

A girl went up to the riverbank where Mangas had entered some hours before—she ducked, unseen, under the flapping crime-scene ribbons and picked up a pendant half-buried in the mud. It was a necklace with the emblem of the river snake. She wept a single tear and resolved to write, one day, about heroes who die with their boots on. Robson Calhoun, the writer, started scribbling his story straight away. He now had a good copy. He wanted to find the right words to do justice to the narrative and to record faithfully the incidents that unfolded on these borders. He knew there were mysteries that might never be explained but his intention was to roll out the story across the universe and condense it like a grain of sand; that wasn't asking too much of his craft, was it? He began his research in the mayor's office. He saw the smashed painting on the floor and used it as his working title: *The Sign of the Broken Hunters*. It would do as a starter.

The *Skanze* continued to blow, for it was wind, you see, but it was more intermittent now, less strong, as if the river gods had been appeased, and the *Wanageeniba*, the river known as *Niba*, gradually settled down again to follow a slightly new course where the pages of new stories could turn with the natural rhythms of the time. They had reached the seventh day since the Lacrosse Festival started so they could all now rest, at last, watching the river flow, feeling the wind brush gently on their faces, granting redemption, perhaps, for as Mayor Frank LeRoy might easily have said, "There's no point swimming against the tide."